GRAY
RESURRECTION

ALAN McDERMOTT
GRAY
RESURRECTION

THOMAS & MERCER

Published by Thomas & Mercer, Seattle

www.apub.com

Amazon, the Amazon logo, and Thomas & Mercer are trademarks of Amazon.com, Inc., or its affiliates.

ISBN-13: 9781477818503
ISBN-10: 1477818502

Cover design by The Book Designers

Library of Congress Control Number: 2013920515

Printed in the United States of America

This book is dedicated to everyone who read and loved Gray Justice.

You guys rock!

Prologue

Friday 13 April 2012

If only he hadn't written that note!

Arlan Banting's infatuation with Maritess Cabanag had been going on for over a year now, and despite being one of the more popular boys in school, he had always been shy around the girls, never comfortable in forming close ties with his female classmates. It had taken months for him to pluck up the courage to invite her to Font's and Mon's Restaurant in Barangay Seaside, and another two weeks to save up enough dinner money to pay for their date, but it had been worth it. He'd discovered that he had more in common with Maritess than he could have ever wished for; they both loved the same music and films, and both played the guitar. Maritess also had the voice of an angel and wrote her own lyrics, which Arlan would put to music before they recorded their efforts on an ancient tape recorder.

One of Arlan's immediate dreams was to buy a decent video camera so that he could record one of their sessions and then send it to all of the many talent shows airing on TV, but having a distinct lack of cash went hand in hand with living in Isabela City.

It had been a first-class city in the early sixties, but after the Moro rebellion razed the plantations it was relegated to a fifth-class province within a decade, and though it had a population of over eighty five thousand people, nobody lived in Isabela City: they simply existed.

Nobody, that is, except the criminal gangs who operated with near-impunity.

They consisted primarily of members of Abu Sayyaf, a military Islamist separatist group operating in Bangsamoro (from the Malay word *Bangsa*, meaning nation of people, and Moro, which refers to the Muslim population of the Philippines). Bangsamoro is an area comprising the Zamboanga Peninsula and the islands of Jolo and Basilan, the capital of which is Isabela City. The gangs controlled everything from the police and local judiciary to protection rackets and drugs, but their main source of income came from kidnapping. They had raised some hefty ransoms over the years, which replaced the donations they'd once received from their Muslim brothers overseas. Al-Qaeda in particular had been only too happy to help in their struggle for an independent province in the early days.

As Arlan strode through the city he regretted his decision to pass the note to Maritess rather than giving it to her after class. If only he'd waited another twenty minutes he wouldn't have been kept behind after school to explain his actions to the principal, and he would have been able to take his normal route home in time to babysit his younger sister while their mother went to her evening job. As it was, the only way he would keep to his schedule was to take a detour down Veterans Avenue. His normal route home took him right at the bandstand followed by a left onto the Rizal Avenue extension, then onto La Piedad and finally down Lower Lanote Road and into a side street where his shanty house sat among a hundred others.

This circuitous route added an extra thirty minutes to his journey home but it meant he could avoid the Jolo Bar, a hangout for members of the Arroyo gang. Unlike the Abu Sayyaf gangs who collected money on behalf of their masters on Jolo Island, the Arroyo gang were in it for themselves. They would sit at the tables outside the bar, drinking San Miguel beer and smoking imported Marlboro cigarettes rather than the much cheaper locally produced version. Anyone who happened within thirty yards of them was fair game, as Arlan had found to his cost earlier that year. A group of five of them had stolen his meagre savings and beaten him for good measure. When his mother had reported the incident to the police they had promised to give it their full attention, then promptly binned the report once she'd left the station.

Like everyone else in Isabela, the police rarely ventured close to the Jolo Bar—unless it was to collect their weekly payoff for turning a blind eye.

Arlan was glad to see that no-one was occupying the chairs outside the bar, but still he quickened his pace, and was about four yards past the entrance when a hand on his shoulder stopped him in his tracks.

'Saan ka pupunta?'

Where do you think you're going?

Arlan knew the answer to the question was nowhere, and he turned to face the man who'd grabbed him. In fact there were four of them, all in their early twenties and most with cigarettes hanging from their mouths. The one with his hand still gripping Arlan's shoulder put his face closer and the stench of stale beer on his breath made Arlan wince. The man's teeth were already in the process of turning brown and Arlan suspected he hadn't seen a tube of toothpaste in his life. He recognised him as the man who had beaten him back in January, and the others had called him Dindo.

'This is our street. You have to pay if you want to walk here.'

Arlan nodded and dug into his pocket, producing his lunch money. He got fifty pesos a day, roughly one US dollar, and for the last few months had managed to save thirty pesos a day towards his camera. He'd spent forty pesos today, deciding to treat himself to a proper lunch, so he thrust the ten peso note towards the man, who sneered at it and swatted it out of his hand.

'You call that payment? What's in the bag?'

'Only my school books, *po*,' Arlan said, using the word to show respect for his elders. He had no respect whatsoever for these people, but if it helped him avoid another beating, it was worth a try.

One of the others grabbed the bag from his shoulder and rummaged through it, throwing out textbooks, pens and pencils. When he came across a photo of Maritess he sniggered and showed it to his friends.

'Who's this? Your sister?'

'No, *po*, my girlfriend.'

'Liar,' Dindo said. 'She's too good for a peasant like you. Maybe you should bring her down to the Jolo and let her meet some real men.'

Dindo grabbed his crotch with his free hand and began rotating his hips back and forth, moaning sounds emanating from his nicotine-stained lips.

Arlan knew a beating was just around the corner, no matter what he did, and the disrespect they were showing towards his first love drove him to actions he'd never considered in his wildest dreams. Before he knew it, his right hand bunched into a fist and flew at Dindo's face, connecting with his left cheek. Unfortunately, Arlan was built for playing the guitar, not street brawling, and the blow bounced off harmlessly. Dindo's face registered shock, not at the force of the impact, but at the sheer impudence of the gutter rat.

'Putang ina mo!! Papatayin kita!!'

But before Dindo could carry out his threat and kill the sonofabitch, someone else had an idea along similar lines, though it was Dindo and his friends who were the targets.

The *jeepney* is the ubiquitous form of public transport in the Philippines. Originally made from surplus jeeps left behind after the Second World War, they were transformed to carry larger numbers of passengers. This particular *jeepney* had been hijacked just a couple of streets away, and as it drove past the Jolo bar four AK-47 rifles appeared through the glassless window on the side of the vehicle and began blazing away at the men standing by the entrance. Despite their aim being below poor, the close proximity guaranteed hits, and the men in the vehicle saw three of their targets fall instantly. Two tried to run but got less than a couple of steps before they too crumpled to the ground.

The *jeepney* stopped and a young man climbed out of the back and strode confidently towards the prostrate figures.

One of them was clawing at the air and begging for help, but mercy and compassion were not in his assailant's vocabulary. Instead, he placed a sheet of paper over his victim's face and used a four-inch knife to staple it to his forehead, before calmly climbing back inside the *jeepney*, banging on the side to tell the driver to move off.

Arlan Banting's last action was to crawl towards the discarded photo of Maritess, the bullet wounds in his chest and arm making it a painful journey. It was inches away from him but every movement sent shockwaves through his body, and when he finally collapsed his finger fell still over her heart.

Chapter One

Saturday 14 April 2012

Sam Grant had become a familiar figure in the Vista Real subdivision on the outskirts of Manila. Having paced out the route from his front door, around the houses and back to his starting position, he knew it was roughly half a mile, and so his aim was to do ten circuits a day.

Almost a year after breaking both legs in the explosion it was a tall ask, but he was determined to get back into the old routine. For the first few days he had jogged round a couple of times before the muscles in his calves screamed for mercy, but a month later he was comfortable at three miles and pushing it at four. An easy five was his ultimate target but he knew that was still a couple of weeks away at least.

After nearly seven laps of the compound the sweat had completely soaked his *sando*, which was the Philippine equivalent of the sleeveless T-shirt. Completing the ensemble were a pair of bright blue shorts and his New Balance sneakers, all of which had been purchased in Manila.

He'd arrived in the country wearing nothing more than a hospital robe and for the first six weeks that was all he'd needed, having been bedridden due to the multiple fractures in his legs. His left arm had also suffered, as had his chest, but it was the face that took the most getting used to. When he'd first seen his new look he had been horrified, but as the swelling from his injuries and the subsequent surgery went down he found himself staring at a totally different person. His eyes seemed sunken due to the heavier brow, and his nose looked like it had been lifted off a local, flat against his face instead of sticking out proudly as it had once done. He had tried growing a full beard to hide the crescent-shaped scar which covered his right cheek but the climate made it itch intolerably, so he settled for a goatee and moustache and simply put up with people staring at it. Time being the healer it was, the scar was already receding, but he knew he would wear it for the rest of his life.

James Farrar had told him to use it as a reminder as to why he was here in the Philippines, but then James Farrar was a dickhead.

From the moment he'd met Farrar, Grant had taken an instant dislike to him. He didn't know if it was the condescending attitude, or the pin-striped suit, or just that he stank of green slime. Of course, he couldn't be sure Farrar was from the Royal Intelligence Corp because one of his favourite games was point-blank refusing to give Grant any information.

After their first brief meeting Farrar had popped by a couple of months later, totally unannounced, just to check on his progress. Since then, he had only made a phone call every couple of months, which suited Grant down to the ground. If Farrar wasn't willing to answer his questions, then the less contact they had, the better.

He waved at Mr Lee as he passed the house on the corner and got a wave in return. The Philippines might not be the most modern country in the world, but the people were generally nice and the whole neighbourhood had made him feel welcome when he'd moved in.

Prior to living here he'd stayed in the house in Subic Freeport, but there was only so much to do there, and he had craved a busier life. On Farrar's second visit he'd requested that a bag of belongings be brought over from the UK. The holdall he'd asked for contained just over a million pounds sterling, the proceeds from the sale of his home and business, and was stored at his solicitor's office in London.

Farrar wasn't pleased at the idea and made his feelings known, but Grant had insisted that he needed his own place to live and money to set up a small business to keep himself occupied. Farrar had eventually relented on the condition that the money be banked and Grant have access to only forty thousand pesos per month. Any withdrawal over that amount would have to be sanctioned by Farrar himself. Grant had agreed, and the bag was delivered to his quarters by diplomatic courier three days later, followed by a phone call from Farrar who took great delight in telling him that the government salary he'd been enjoying was coming to an end, since he was now able to support himself. Grant wasn't even slightly concerned at losing the miserly allowance and told Farrar as much, causing even greater animosity between the pair.

The house he'd bought, with Farrar's consent, was a two bedroom up and down, with a decent garden and covered car port. He could have bought something ten times the size and still have had half of his money in the bank, but as he was going to be living alone he didn't see the point.

As he approached his house he saw Alma appear from the front door, hosepipe in her hand ready to water the plants. He blew her a kiss as he passed and continued round the corner and onto lap eight.

Alma had happened out of the blue, and it had been the last thing he'd expected.

He'd been out shopping for kitchen appliances for his new home when she'd caught his eye, and he'd found himself smiling at her. More surprisingly, she'd smiled back from behind the counter and before he'd even thought about it he'd found himself standing before her, lost for words. Then came the realisation that she might have been smiling simply because that was what she was paid to do: put on her customer service face.

'Um, I'm looking for a washing machine,' he had said feebly.

The smile had remained in place, and the amount of eye contact he'd got went well beyond customer care, so he'd chanced his arm and invited her for a coffee after work. She'd readily accepted, which he'd found amazing, and after they had arranged a time for him to pick her up, he'd left the shop looking for the hidden cameras, convinced it was some kind of sick reality TV gag.

He'd then walked straight back in and purchased the white goods he'd originally gone in for.

The date at a local coffee shop had gone well. Alma spoke English very well, although there was a hint of an American accent, a result of the US presence up until November 1992, when the American flag was finally lowered in Subic for the last time.

He'd been conscious of his looks all evening, though Alma either hadn't noticed or hadn't cared. She'd wanted to know about his past, and he'd had to think quickly.

A year earlier he'd been Tom Gray, widower. A few weeks later he was Tom Gray, terrorist. The next thing he knew he was waking up in an Admiral's bedroom in the Philippines with a new name, a new face and an explicit warning from Farrar: tell anyone about his previous life and he would be dead within twenty-four hours. So he'd spent the evening telling her about Sam Grant, entrepreneur.

The story he'd told was of a man who'd lived in London all his life, taking various part-time jobs before starting his own small business selling T-shirts online. A raft of other websites soon sprang up, and it was while on holiday in Manila the previous year that he'd seen the lack of online shopping sites and decided to corner the market.

The latter part was true, as he'd tried to order some sneakers over the Internet and found it impossible, so he'd rented an office, furnished it with half a dozen computers and hired some developers to create the sites. He now had a dozen customers signed up to sell their goods through his web portals, offering them the software and hosting for free in exchange for five percent of each sale.

Sales had taken a while to pick up, he'd explained to her, but the business was starting to pay for itself.

He'd been in the process of creating the warehouse and distribution side of the business when he'd met Alma. She was twenty-seven and had been working in the department store for a couple of years, having travelled up from the southern islands to stay with relatives in Manila, and having previously worked in a wholesale company she had plenty of contacts that would help him in his quest to start selling direct to the public. That revelation had prompted him to offer her a job with his company at double her current wages, and she had accepted without a moment's hesitation.

They'd parted that evening without so much as a goodnight kiss, Grant heeding the words of an ex-pat he'd met in a bar when he'd first arrived in Manila.

'It takes time to court a good Filipina,' he'd said. 'You should never try anything on the first three dates.'

It wasn't until he'd got into the taxi to take him home that Grant had thought about his wife and son. Was he being disrespectful towards them by flirting with another woman? All it had been was coffee and a chat, yet deep down he knew that he wanted a whole lot more.

He'd wrestled with his conscience during the days leading up to their second date, and had come clean with Alma about the fact that he had been previously married. He'd lied when he'd said wife and child had both died in a car crash several years earlier, but at least she now knew about them.

It wasn't the third but the fifth date before he kissed her, by which time he'd come to terms with the fact that he had to move on, no matter how much he missed his family. Their relationship had moved on at an advanced pace from that first kiss, with consummation following soon after and Alma moving in with him a few weeks later.

She had certainly made her mark on the house, adding a woman's touch to his barrack-style minimalism. Pictures now adorned the walls and a sensible spread of ornaments brightened up the living room. She had also introduced him to Filipino cooking in a big way, with *Sinigang Na Hipon*, fresh prawns and vegetables in a sour tamarind broth being his favourite dish. The food had certainly piled on the pounds, which was one of the reasons he wanted to get back into his five-miles-a-day routine.

The muscles in his calves were beginning to cramp as he neared the end of the eighth lap but he felt confident that he could get another in before calling it a day. He tried to ignore the pain as he pounded the road, instead reflecting on the great shape his new life was taking. All would be wonderful if he could just cut James Farrar out of it.

He turned the corner into his street and saw the black SUV parked up in his driveway, and he used that as an excuse to cut his exercise short. As he strolled up to the vehicle the driver's side window hummed as it descended and Farrar's face appeared, looking ridiculous in aviator sunglasses.

Speak of the devil, Grant thought, *and his shit-filled illegitimate son will appear.*

'Get in,' Farrar said, polite as ever.

Grant climbed into the passenger seat and the blast from the car's air con hit him like a frozen sledgehammer, chilling him to the bone—much to Farrar's delight. Grant appreciated air conditioning and had it in every room in his home, but nothing as ferocious as this.

'We have some work for you,' Farrar said without preamble.

'What kind of work?'

'I'll give you the details later. Just be ready to board a plane in five days' time. That should give you plenty of time to sort out your affairs here.'

Grant stared at him for a moment, the anger building.

'No thanks,' he finally said, and made to open the door. Farrar was apoplectic.

'What do you mean "No"? You'll do as you're damn well told.'

Grant turned back to him. 'Not until I get some answers.'

'Such as ...?'

'I want to know who I'm working for.'

'You are working for Her Majesty's government.'

'I gathered that, but which branch?' Grant asked, exasperated.

'That's need-to-know.'

'Yes, and I need to fucking know.'

'No you don't,' Farrar said. 'All you have to do is follow instructions. Now, there are rumblings of terror cells operating in Europe and we want you to go and do what you do best.'

'You're not listening, Farrar. I want some answers before I do anything for you.'

Farrar sighed and angled himself to get a better view of Grant. 'It wouldn't do you any good to know who my bosses are. We're so black, even the prime minister doesn't know the full extent of what we do, and you won't find us in the Yellow Pages. All you need to know is that we are the cutting edge of anti-terrorism and we have a proactive agenda. We like to stop attacks while they are in the planning stage, and do it in such a way that they don't know that we know, if you know what I mean.'

Grant's expression barely changed as he waited for Farrar to elaborate.

'We take down cells at the earliest possible stage, causing accidents so that the men at the top don't know we're on to them. Their people die in car crashes, in street robberies, all manner of different ways, but crucially they are explainable accidents.

However, you can only have so many of your people die in a crash before it becomes suspicious, and so we need to think of more ingenious ways. That's where you come in.

'Your little stunt last year was well thought out, and we need that kind of lateral thinking to enable us to ramp up the body count. We're taking down our fair share of terrorists, don't get me wrong, but there are just too many others willing to replace them.'

'Then go for the main men, not the foot soldiers,' Grant said. Despite his reticence to engage in conversation with the man, his training and planning skills kicking in before he had a chance to stop himself.

'You see, that's what I mean. You hear the problem and immediately have the solution.'

'Don't try and blow smoke up my arse; it won't work. Besides, I'm out of that whole business now. You'll have to find someone else.'

'This isn't up for discussion, Sam. You either do as we ask, or things get very uncomfortable for you.'

'What are you going to do?' Grant laughed. 'Come and visit me every day? I'm a free man.'

'I was thinking more of having the lease on your company offices cancelled, or maybe retracting your Barangay clearance to operate a business. That puts your staff out of work and your business goes down the pan. I can also stop all withdrawals from your bank account, leaving you without a pot to piss in.'

Farrar nodded toward Alma, who was just finishing up with the hose. 'Do you really think your dolly bird will hang around when she finds out you can't support her anymore?'

He enjoyed the pained look on Grant's face at the thought of losing his bed warmer, a look that swiftly turned to anger.

'I'll do one job, but with conditions,' Grant said, more than a touch of hostility in his voice. Farrar started to object but Grant cut him off. 'I want some of my old team with me. Sonny Baines, Len

Smart and Tristram Barker-Fink all helped come up with the plan last year, and I want their help again.'

'Impossible. The fewer people involved the better.'

'It's not negotiable, Farrar. As you've already said, they don't need to know who they're working for; they just need to follow instructions. I'm sure you'll have front companies that can employ them at proper contractor rates, so make it happen.'

Farrar wasn't accustomed to having people dictate terms to him, and was determined to make that clear. 'It's out of the question. We have no idea where these people are. It could take weeks to track them down.'

'That's bullshit. I could call their mobiles and be talking to them in a couple of minutes. The only reason I haven't spoken to them in the last year is because you told me not to. I've done everything you asked of me, so it's time you gave me something in return.'

Farrar considered the request a little more and decided the time was right to accede to Grant's demand. 'Okay, you can have Smart and Baines. Unfortunately, Tristram bought it in Iraq a few months ago.'

'How?'

'I don't have all the details,' Farrar said. 'All I know is he was doing some bodyguard work and his client was attacked by a large force. The agency he worked for couldn't give us any further information.'

Grant gazed out of the window, staring at nothing in particular as he thought about his good friend. Tris had served with him in the regiment and they had shared a couple of tours in Iraq, and Grant had subsequently hired him when he was managing director of Viking Security Services. When Grant—in his previous incarnation as Tom Gray—had first come up with the notion of kidnapping five habitual criminals in order to force the government to come down harder on repeat offenders, it was Tris who had been the most supportive, helping mould the initial spur-of-the-moment idea into a solid, viable plan. Tris had also been one of the people to administer CPR when he'd been seriously injured in the explosion that had brought his four-day siege to an abrupt end, and he had never been able to thank him.

In fact, Grant hadn't spoken to any of his friends since his arrival in the Philippines. He'd been tempted, obviously, but he knew that Farrar would be monitoring all of their incoming calls. If he'd tried to contact them, Farrar would have known about it.

Farrar's main concern, however, was that Grant might reveal the fact that he was actually Tom Gray, a man for whom the people of Britain had held a two-week protest demanding his release from custody. The official line was that Tom Gray had died from his injuries, when in fact he had been spirited out of the country to prevent him causing the government any further embarrassment. Grant had long ago considered the implications should the world find out that Tom Gray was still alive, and it didn't look rosy. Farrar would certainly follow through with his earlier threat to have him killed, at the very least. He might even go as far as to terminate all others who knew about him, and that included some good friends back in England.

Although he hadn't asked to be placed in this predicament, Sam Grant knew he had to deal with it, and had been doing quite a good job up until the last few minutes.

He turned back to Farrar, a steely look in his eyes. 'I want Sonny and Len here before we set off, plus full details of the operation. We'll travel together and I'll brief them on the journey.'

'Don't push your luck, Sam. You may be good at what you do, but you're not indispensable.'

They sat staring at each other for a full minute, and it was Farrar who backed down first. 'Okay, I'll give you the details on Monday and get Baines and Smart here by Tuesday evening. Just be ready to fly on Thursday afternoon.'

'How long will I be gone?'

'It shouldn't take more than a couple of weeks. It all depends on how quickly you can devise and then execute your plan. We'll give you the target, you do the rest.'

Grant nodded and opened the door, glad to get back out into the warm evening air. He didn't look back as he headed towards the house and he heard Farrar reverse off the driveway and disappear towards the subdivision gates.

Inside the house he found Alma preparing *pulutan* for the evening's game of *Tong-its*, a rummy-like card game the locals enjoyed playing, especially for money. The stakes were never high but it made for a good night's entertainment, particularly when accompanied by a few San Miguel beers, his neighbours and a table full of *pulutan*, drinking-food to soak up the alcohol. Grant had always been one to drink first and eat later, but he had slipped comfortably into the habit of picking at the array of small dishes throughout a drinking session. Popular dishes included *Sisig*, which consisted of ground pigs' ears and liver, and *Tokwa't Baboy*, toasted tofu and boiled ham in garlic-flavoured soy sauce. Alma had become famous with the local men for her generous servings, and there was never an empty chair on card night at the Grant household.

Grant hugged Alma from behind as she washed the rice in a large pan to get rid of the starch. He stood a good eighteen inches taller than her, and had to stoop to kiss her affectionately on the neck. He then checked the supply of San Miguel and saw that he was down to less than a crate, so he grabbed a five-hundred peso note and headed towards the door.

'Just gonna get some more beer,' he told her, and got a smile in reply.

Like many Filipinas, Alma didn't drink; they tended to leave that to the Filipino men. She enjoyed the card evenings immensely, though, as it meant the wives would join their husbands in the house. The men would sit out in the garden while the ladies spent the evening inside, usually doing cross-stitch while sharing the week's gossip.

Grant returned from the local shop within five minutes, his arms straining under the weight of two crates of San Miguel. The beers went into the drinks fridge, which he'd bought specifically for Saturday nights, and then he headed to the bathroom to have a shower.

The guests began arriving just after eight that evening, with Mr Lee the first as always.

'Sam, how are you? How's business?'

'Booming,' Grant said. 'How's the Lee empire coming along?'

Albert Lee had a string of shops in all the major malls dotted throughout Manila, and seemed to open a new one every time they met. 'I'm meeting with two companies next week. If either of them can provide a suitable delivery service I will be in a position to sign up to your website.'

Grant was happy at the news, but it reminded him that he had to make arrangements for his office manager, Alfredo, to take over for a fortnight. He also had to break the news to Alma, but thought it best to wait until they were alone.

The evening began well, with each of the five guests doing their best to outdo each other in the business stakes. One would announce that he had secured a new contract with a major supplier, and another would trump that with an international order. The banter was light-hearted, but Grant wondered if they would put so much effort into their work if they didn't have their Saturday night bragging rights to look forward to.

Grant himself wasn't one for getting into pissing contests, no matter how good-natured, so he settled for soaking up information about the current trading conditions. He'd just learned of a new competitor in the online market who had been canvassing his friends when the need to pee grabbed him, so he excused himself and made his way to the CR, or Comfort Room, the Filipino term for the toilet. On his way past the living room he saw Alma in tears, being comforted by her friends.

'What's wrong?' he asked, taking a seat next to her, but Alma was too consumed with grief to answer.

'Her brother died today,' a friend said. 'She just got a phone call from her mother.'

Grant wrapped his arms around Alma and hugged her tight. He knew she had a brother and a much younger sister as she was always talking about them, and was always sending a few pesos home to help them out. She was so proud of her brother for being near the top of his class despite his poor background, and now that bright light had been extinguished.

'How did it happen?' Grant asked her friends in a hushed voice, but all he got was shrugs in response. He wasn't about to push Alma in her present state, so he let the question lie. A friend appeared with a glass of water and Grant offered her the seat next to his girlfriend, then he went outside to call an early end to the game.

His guests were understanding and went inside to offer Alma their support, but by this time she had regained a little control and assured them she would be okay. After making some more consoling noises their friends began to drift off into the night, leaving the couple alone.

Alma began to open up, and she replayed the brief conversation she'd had with her mother. 'Arlan didn't come home from school at the usual time and Mama was really angry. She thought he'd gone out with his girlfriend, but when Maritess called asking to speak to him she got worried and called the police. That was when she found out that he'd been shot. The police said it was a robbery, but Arlan had nothing worth stealing...'

Her words tapered off as the tears came again, and just after midnight she finally drifted off to sleep in his arms.

Chapter Two

Sunday 15 April 2012

Grant woke up on the sofa alone, a thin ray of sunlight blinding him as it broke through a gap in the curtains. He immediately remembered the events of the previous evening and went in search of Alma, eventually finding her in their bedroom. She was packing a holdall with clothes and a few toiletries and she looked up at him as he appeared in the doorway, her eyes still red.

'Kumusta?' he asked.

'I'm okay,' she said, resuming her packing. 'But I have to go home for the funeral. I'll be back in a couple of days.'

Grant moved into the room and gave her a hug. 'I understand. I'll come with you.'

'Are you sure? What about the office? Who will run things while you're gone?'

'It's fine. Alfredo can manage.'

'It's not really safe in Isabela City,' Alma said, concern etched on her face. 'Maybe you should stay here, I'll be back soon.'

'Darling, if it isn't safe, I'm definitely coming.'

Alma smiled and kissed him on the cheek.

'How do we get there?' Grant asked her.

'We can take a flight to Zamboanga City and then take the boat across the Basilan Strait to Isabela. There's a plane leaving just after two this afternoon.'

Grant checked his watch, added on three hours to get through the Manila traffic and realised he only had an hour and a half to get ready. 'Call and book the tickets and a taxi,' he said. 'I'll go and take a shower.'

He finished washing in less than five minutes and as he dried himself he realised he would have to call Farrar to let him know where he was going. After getting dressed he punched the speed-dial number and the call was answered on the second ring.

'What?'

There's no end to this guy's manners, Grant thought. 'I'm taking off for a few days,' he replied. 'I should be back late Tuesday night, maybe Wednesday.'

'Taking off? Where to? This is no time for a holiday!'

Grant explained the situation but Farrar was unfazed by the news. 'My condolences and all that, but you're staying put. She can go down there herself.'

'I wasn't calling to ask your permission; I'm letting you know so that you can tell Len and Sonny that the key to my house will be with my next-door neighbour. Tell Sonny to introduce himself as cousin Bob and they can make themselves comfortable until I get back.'

'You really are the most insolent, jumped-up —'

Grant ended the call and turned the phone off. He considered leaving it in the house while he was away, but he needed to be available should Alfredo have any problems at the office, so he tucked it into his jeans and began filling his sports bag with enough clothes for three days. In went socks, underpants, T-shirts and shorts, along with a spare pair of jeans and his toiletries: shaving kit; toothbrush and toothpaste; and soap. The final item was his bottle of Off Lotion insect repellent.

Farrar might be an arsehole, but he was right about the bloody mosquitoes.

The taxi arrived early to take them to Ninoy Aquino airport, which was just as well as traffic was exceptionally heavy, even for

Manila. They got to the Cebu Pacific Air desk and picked up their tickets with a couple of minutes to spare, then rushed through the departure lounge to the boarding gate.

Grant was glad to see that the plane was an Airbus A319 rather than some ten-seater turbo-prop, and he enjoyed a snack on the flight, his first bite of the day.

An hour and a half later they arrived in Zamboanga City and took a taxi to the port, where Grant opted for the MS Weesam Express as it took just forty-five minutes to make the crossing and had air conditioning, as opposed to the normal ferry which took an hour longer and would leave him at the mercy of the late afternoon sun.

Once they disembarked they had a choice of vehicles to take them to their destination. Grant declined the offer of bicycles and motorcycles, both with sidecars capable of carrying two passengers, and chose instead to splash out an extra hundred pesos on a taxi.

The journey to the house where Alma had grown up took just fifteen minutes, and as with the rest of the journey she sat in silence, looking out of the side window at nothing in particular. He did the same, not wanting to interrupt her thoughts, knowing full well what she was going through. It was almost two years since his son had died at the hands of a car thief, and less than a year later he had lost his wife, too, so he appreciated that there were moments when it was appropriate to talk and times when he should leave her to her reflections.

The only time she spoke was towards the end of their journey.

'Mama doesn't know about ... us,' she told him. 'Can I introduce you as my boss?'

Grant assured her he was fine with that, but pointed out that it would be awkward if they were going to sleep under the same roof. Alma hadn't thought that far ahead, and was grateful when he offered to stay at a local hotel.

When they arrived at their destination he was surprised to see around thirty people sitting outside in the street. Most were playing cards, piles of money in the middle of the tables. The house itself was more like an old allotment shed, with the front wall made of two wooden doors nailed horizontally onto a makeshift frame. The inside was no better: the floor was bare concrete; cheap plasterboard lined the internal walls; and the only sign of technology was a portable television on a wooden sideboard.

In the centre of the small living room a couple of tables had been shoved together and on top was an open casket. Toddlers were chasing each other around it, laughing and giggling, while parents sat around the edge of the room chatting and eating. In the small kitchen towards the back of the house three women were preparing yet more food, and looking round he wondered where they could possibly put it. Every available inch of space was already taken up with bowls of rice; pork, chicken and fish dishes; and copious amounts of soft drinks.

Alma was staring at the peaceful face of her sibling when a woman in her late forties entered the room and came towards them.

Alma threw her arms around her. 'Mama.'

They hugged for some time before Alma's mother noticed the stranger staring at them. Introductions were made and Grant found that she spoke very little English, but Alma translated and Grant replied with some of the Tagalog phrases he had learnt over the last few months.

A plate heaped with rice and pork was suddenly thrust into his hand and he was ushered outside to a spare seat. Alma remained inside to catch up with her family, so he got stuck in. One of the locals at the table spoke passable English and sparked up a conversation, though Grant was more interested in the food than chit-chat. He answered questions about his past as truthfully as he could, though at times he had to be economical with his words.

A police car pulled up and he watched the sole occupant get out. He gave Grant a curious glance as he passed, then walked into the house. Through the open door Sam saw him cuddle Alma, a little too passionately for his liking, so he polished off his food and went inside on the pretence of grabbing a second helping. Alma stopped him on his way to the table and introduced the officer.

'This is Lorenzo,' she said. 'We went to school together.'

Grant shook his hand. 'Sam,' he smiled, wondering what it was they'd done together *after* school.

'Lorenzo was just telling me that Arlan wasn't killed in a robbery.'

The officer gestured for her to keep her voice down. 'That's what I believe,' he said softly. 'There was a message attached to one of the other victims which tells me he was caught up in a gang war.'

'Arlan wasn't in a gang,' Alma said with indignation.

'I know. We think he was just in the wrong place at the wrong time.'

'What was the message?' Grant asked.

'It said "Basilan belongs to Abu Sayyaf".'

'Who's he?'

'Not a *he*,' Alma said. 'Abu Sayyaf is a Muslim independence group.'

'More like terrorists,' Lorenzo said. 'And they want complete control of the region. There have been many gang killings in the last few months and we believe they want to eliminate all of their competition.'

'But why was Arlan's death reported as a robbery?' Grant asked.

'Because certain members of the police would prefer that Abu Sayyaf incidents are not reported to the mainland. It might affect their income.'

'I don't understand.'

'The senior police officers receive payments from Abu Sayyaf and turn a blind eye to their activities,' Lorenzo said. 'Their crimes are attributed to others and they are allowed to operate as they wish.'

'Are all policemen on the payroll?' Grant asked Lorenzo quizzically, and the Filipino resented the suggestion.

'No,' he said, a little too loudly, drawing looks from others in the room. He noticed the attention and dropped his voice a little. 'Some of us actually believe in the role we've been given. That's why I wanted Alma to know the truth.' He looked at both of them in turn. 'Don't tell anyone what I just told you.'

Grant and Alma nodded solemnly.

'Where are you staying in Isabela?' Lorenzo asked him, his voice back to its normal level.

'I was hoping to find a hotel for a couple of days,' Grant said, although sensing a history between these two he was no longer sure he wanted to let Alma out of his sight.

'I know a good hotel not far from here,' Lorenzo said. 'I can take you if you like, but we have to be quick; the reception closes early.'

Grant looked at Alma and she nodded at him. 'Go, I'll come and get you in the morning.'

He grabbed his bag and followed Lorenzo to the car, and as they pulled away he looked back at the house and saw Alma in the doorway, offering a surreptitious wave which he returned through the open window.

'Alma tells me she works for you,' Lorenzo said as they drove sedately through the evening traffic. 'What does your company do?'

'We build websites for online shopping.'

The concept was lost on the policeman, so Grant explained the principle.

'Does it make a lot of money?' Lorenzo asked.

'At the moment we only make about a million pesos a month, which is just about enough to break even. Hopefully we can start showing a healthy profit in the next twelve months.'

Lorenzo whistled, impressed with the figures although he didn't appreciate the fact that it barely covered Grant's outgoings. The numbers were still going round in his mind as he helped Grant check in to the hotel, and after he made a mental note of the room number he left his charge to settle in for the evening.

'I suggest you stay in your room tonight,' he told Grant. 'The streets of Isabela are not safe for a stranger, especially after dark. Abu Sayyaf are everywhere, and you would make a good trophy for them.'

Grant agreed to the suggestion. He took the stairs to the first floor and found room one zero eight, and once inside he realised that his idea of 'good' differed hugely from Lorenzo's. The bedding had seen better days—not to mention a lot fewer stains—and the toilet was functional in that there was a pot to sit on but no cistern to flush his bodily fluids away. Instead, a bucket full of water and a large ladle had been provided. His morning ritual for the next couple of days would consist of shit, scoop, shower and shave.

The television offered only local channels, so he settled on the bed, wishing he'd brought a book along, but at the same time thankful for the insect repellent.

In the street below, Lorenzo sat in the patrol car looking up at the second floor. He toyed with the phone in his hand as he wondered what exactly there was between his old girlfriend and this foreigner. It didn't make sense for a company owner to accompany a member of staff to their home town for a funeral unless it was more than just a working relationship.

When Alma had announced that she was going to Manila to stay with family just after her twenty-fifth birthday he had been devastated. He had been trying to cultivate a romance between them for the previous three years, building on their friendship. He would visit her in the evenings and often bring his guitar to jam with Arlan, though she rarely took up his offer to meet on the weekends, insisting that was family time.

Then she'd dropped the bombshell, dashing all of his dreams. He'd tried to persuade her not to go, to stay with him, but she'd wanted more for her family and saw Manila as the place to find a better opportunity. He'd relented after a while, convincing himself that she would be back within a few weeks, but as the months wore on her letters told him she was doing well and really enjoying the new challenge. Whenever he had written to her he'd casually joked about her new man but she had always assured him that she wasn't looking for a boyfriend.

That was, until three months ago.

Her letters had suddenly become less frequent and a lot shorter, until they had stopped completely four weeks ago. Now she was back, and with a foreigner in tow.

He had told the truth when he'd told Sam that he hadn't taken bribes from Abu Sayyaf.

However, there was always a first time.

He punched in a number and waited a moment for the recipient to pick up.

'*Pare*, I have something you might be interested in ...'

Chapter Three

Monday 16 April 2012

Grant didn't know if it was the lack of air conditioning or the food he'd eaten at Alma's house, but he woke up just after midnight covered in sweat, the thin cotton bed sheet sticking to his naked body. He headed into the bathroom and stood under the weak shower, allowing the tepid water to slowly wash away the layer of perspiration. As he dried himself he realised after five minutes that he was no longer towelling off water: he was back to the layer of sweat that had replaced it. Giving up on the fruitless exercise, he walked back into the bedroom where he grabbed a local newspaper and used it to fan himself.

He turned on the television, knowing that trying to get back to sleep would be futile. The music from a talent show blasted into the room and he jumped for the remote, turning the volume down to an acceptable level. After flicking through the channels he settled on cock fighting, although he saw more adverts than action. That was the trouble with TV in the Philippines: they showed four minutes of the programme followed by five minutes of advertisements.

Grant was just learning how to get bigger breasts when he heard a knock at the door and he immediately assumed it was someone coming to complain about the television being too loud. He dashed into the toilet and grabbed a towel to wrap around his waist, then opened the door a little and peered through the crack. As he did so he was shoved backwards and four men ran into the room, weapons raised and pointing at him. Two of the men had handguns, the other two rifles which he recognised as American M16s.

'On the floor!' one shouted. Gray complied, a little too slowly for their liking, and he got a rifle butt in the shoulder for his troubles. He sank to his knees, still holding the towel, and weighed up the men before him.

Three of them were about five feet six tall, about average for Filipinos, while the one who'd struck him dwarfed them by a good fourteen inches. The rifle looked like a toy in his huge hands and he was the only one without facial hair. Grant decided to designate him 'Ox', because the dumb-looking giant probably couldn't spell it, but he looked like he could lift one.

Grant considered fighting his way out, but they had too much distance between them, whether by training or chance, he didn't know. Any attempt to take one of their weapons would afford the others enough time to give him the bad news, so he decided to wait and see what they wanted. The longer he managed to play this out, the more he could learn about them, in particular their strengths and weaknesses.

It didn't take long for them to reveal the reason for the visit.

'We are Abu Sayyaf,' one of them said, and Grant decided he was the leader of the little group. 'You will come with us.'

'What for?' Grant asked, feigning fear. Back in his Army days he'd been taught that by acting submissively in these situations his enemies would most likely be more lenient, whereas someone who was antagonistic would be watched more closely and treated with more aggression.

'You will be our hostage. You are a rich man and will pay us a million dollars.'

'I haven't got a million dollars,' Grant said, incredulous. 'I just work in an office.'

'Liar!' The shout was punctuated with another blow from the rifle butt, this time to the back of the head. He collapsed, his vision blurred and bells ringing in his ears. 'We know you are a business-man and have a company in Manila. You will pay us!'

One of the men grabbed his clothes from the chair and threw them at him.

'Put your clothes on,' Leader shouted, while another emptied Grant's bag out onto the bed. After handing the mobile over to his boss he put the rest of the belongings back in the bag and swung it over his shoulder.

Grant dressed slowly despite their prompting, pretending to fumble with his clothes as he desperately thought of a way out. Leader had backed away to the door, covering him with his pistol, and Grant realised that there would be no escape while they were in the room. The situation got worse a moment later.

'Anton, tie his hands,' Leader said, and one of the men stepped forward and produced something from his pocket. It looked to Grant like the flex from a lamp, and he put his hands out, palms facing each other. Anton was having none of it, and he gestured with his own hands to show that he wanted Grant to place one wrist on top of the other. *These guys have had practice*, Grant thought as he followed Anton's instructions.

With his hands secure they ushered him into the hallway, but even here they were too spread out for him to take them all down, even if his hands had been free. Once down the stairs he saw that the reception desk was empty, and Ox used the muzzle of his rifle to urge Grant through the front door where a battered Toyota saloon was waiting.

Leader opened the boot and told him to climb inside, and he looked round for a possible alternative. There was a sprinkling of people on the streets and he considered crying out for help, but his captors were either blissfully unaware of the onlookers or, more ominously, they didn't care. If it was the latter, then attracting their attention was unlikely to do him any good, so he complied once more.

The lid slammed down, blotting out the meagre street lighting. The air inside the cramped compartment was stifling. The car then took off and his whole body rattled as they navigated the uneven streets, his head crashing against the lid of the boot every time they hit a pothole. By the time they reached the outskirts of town a trickle of blood was already running down his forehead, and things only got worse once they hit the dirt roads leading out of Isabela City.

Grant knew the situation wasn't going to improve anytime soon, but one advantage he had was that they didn't know about his military past. They thought he was just a businessman, and he would happily keep up that illusion until the time came.

The pace of the car slowed but the jostling continued for another thirty minutes, then abruptly stopped. Grant heard and felt the occupants climbing out and the doors slamming shut, and a moment later the boot was opened. Grant closed one eye to protect his night vision, expecting light to come flooding in, but the night was pitch black. As he was being dragged out of the car he realised that the reason for the utter darkness was that they had driven deep into the jungle, and not even the night stars could penetrate the tree tops.

Blood dripped from his forehead into his eyes and he wiped it away with his wrist. He then stretched his legs, glad of the chance to straighten them again after his short confinement, but no sooner had he got the circulation going than Ox once more prodded him with the rifle, suggesting he fall in behind Leader, who was striding into the darkness. As he set off, the lights of the car lit the men up, then reversed and disappeared back in the direction of the main town.

'Emilio, you watch our backs,' Anton said as he fell in behind his giant comrade.

After those few words they walked in silence for three hours, fording a shallow stream before heading to higher ground where the going was tougher on Grant. His calves began to burn as they took a circuitous route up the hill but fortunately Leader was also in the mood for a break and ordered everyone to rest up. While his captors dumped their gear and sought a comfortable place to sit, Grant collapsed into the foliage and began massaging his legs. He hadn't had a drink of water in hours and knew from his jungle training days in the regiment that dehydration was his most dangerous enemy right now. Unless he got that under control he would be in no fit state to walk much further, never mind find a way to escape.

'I need a drink,' he shouted over to Leader, who immediately came over and clamped a hand over his mouth.

'Keep your voice down. The *sundalos* are everywhere.'

Grant waited until the sweaty palm had been removed then asked what *sundalos* were, a lot more quietly this time.

'They are the Armed Forces of the Philippines. They want to deny us our right to an independent Muslim state.'

Grant was encouraged by the fact that they were surrounded by the Army and it showed on his face, but his hopes were soon dashed.

'They are incompetent, but even an idiot with a gun can be dangerous. They don't care who they shoot at, as long as they fire in our general direction. Sometimes they hit us, sometimes our hostages. I don't think you should look at them as your saviours; they are more likely to kill you than rescue you.'

With a grin, Leader returned to his small backpack and took a swig from a half-full bottle of water before throwing it over to Grant, who gulped it down. It was warm and did little to quench his thirst, but it would keep him going for an hour or two.

A few minutes later they heard faint voices coming from below them on the hill, and Leader whispered for everyone to start moving again. No-one was sure if the voices belonged to soldiers or civilians but they were taking no chances, and climbed ever higher while making as little sound as possible. Even Grant, who would have been as clumsy as possible if it meant alerting a rescue team, did his best to keep the noise to a minimum.

They trudged on for another two hours until Leader suddenly raised his hand for those behind him to stop. Everyone dropped to a knee, even Grant. He cursed himself for letting his training take over but none of the others seemed to care; they were more intent on finding out what Leader had come across.

After an interminable three minutes Leader stood again and opened his arms. From the darkness two men appeared, both carrying rifles, and they each hugged Leader.

'*Salam alaikum*!' they said as they kissed each other on both cheeks. Grant's guards joined in the greetings and when they'd finished one of the newcomers came and stood over him. He considered Grant for a moment and then rattled off some Tagalog to his companions. They grabbed Grant under his arms and lifted him to his feet, then pushed him forward. Once again Leader took point and it was only a few minutes later that they arrived in the camp.

In fact, the camp was little more than a clearing in the jungle, the remnants of the smaller trees they'd chopped down to create it still littering the ground. Larger trees were dotted around the centre and all of them had hammocks swinging between them, some with more than one occupant. Over to Grant's right he saw a small tent capable of housing two, maybe three people at a push, and to his left he saw a group huddled together on the ground.

There were four Filipinos, a Chinese couple and three westerners, and Ox poked him with his rifle, gesturing that he should join them. He took a seat next to the white trio and the first thing he noticed was their poor condition. The two males were undernourished, their faces having an almost skeletal appearance.

Both wore shorts and T-shirts which looked like they hadn't been washed in months and one man had a festering sore the size of a golf ball on his neck. The woman seemed in better health, though her clothes were just as ragged. Her shoulder-length blonde hair fell about her face and clearly hadn't seen shampoo in a long time, but underneath all the dirt he could see a rather striking woman. Despite his circumstances something stirred inside him, something he hadn't felt in years.

She grabbed his arms, her grip surprisingly strong.

'I'm Vick,' she said. 'Vick Phillips.'

'Vick?' Grant looked confused.

'Short for Victoria,' she explained.

'Ah, I see. Sam. Sam Grant. How long have you all been here?'

Vick gestured to the men. 'Robert Moore and I have been here since January and Eddie Halton arrived about three weeks later.'

'What about the others?' he asked, looking beyond the trio.

'The Chinese couple have been here for about two months and don't speak a word of English, and the Filipinos ...'

Her words drifted off and her eyes glazed over as she stared towards the rising sun as it broke the horizon.

'The locals don't have the same value as we do,' Moore explained. 'They tend to have a couple of weeks to come up with payment or they are just taken away and never come back. We heard one of the guards joking about how one man's head bounced and rolled down the hill. That seems to be their favourite way of dealing with people.'

No wonder they all look petrified, Grant thought. He wasn't afraid of death, but he didn't like the idea of it coming by decapitation.

'Have you heard anything about us?' Vick asked. 'On the news, I mean?'

'I don't really follow the local news. I mostly read the BBC news website.'

Vick looked at him, imploring him to continue.

'Sorry, but I haven't seen anything about you, any of you. Are you sure the government know you're here?'

'Of course they do. We spoke to the British Embassy the day we were kidnapped and Jonjon has sent them messages every week.'

There was no way of sugar coating it, so Grant settled for: 'I'm sorry ...'

An awkward silence followed, during which Grant took the opportunity to assess his captors. There were fifteen guards that he could see, some adorned in US Army combat trousers, boots and smocks while others wore a mishmash of army gear and civvies. He didn't see anyone who looked over the age of thirty, and three of them looked like they should still be in school. Two things they all had in common were that they wore bandanas in varying shades of red and each carried small arms, including M16 rifles and pistols. Almost all had *bolos*—long knives similar to machetes and used for hacking a path through the jungle—hanging from their waists. A couple even had hand grenades dangling from various bits of webbing. A couple of multi-shot Soviet RPG-7s were propped up against a tree next to a box of high explosive rounds, representing their heavy arsenal.

'We'll be moving out soon,' Vick said, watching the Abu Sayyaf members pull down their hammocks and gather their belongings.

'Where are we going?'

'Somewhere else,' she said flatly. 'We never have a destination, we just march until sundown.'

That made sense to Grant. Alma had told him that the island of Basilan was only about forty miles across, and with the AFP constantly hounding them Abu Sayyaf would have to stay mobile to avoid detection.

His stomach growled and he realised that he hadn't had a bite to eat since the previous evening. 'What about breakfast?' he asked. 'Have you already eaten?'

'Ha!' Halton snorted. 'We're lucky to get a handful of rice once a day. Once we had a tin of sardines between twelve of us and we thought it was Christmas and our birthdays all rolled into one.'

His accent marked him as American, whereas Grant could tell that Vick and Moore were definitely British.

'And now that you've joined us,' Halton continued, 'our portion just got smaller.'

'I don't think Sam chose to be here, Eddie,' Vick chastised. 'Given the choice, I'm sure he would prefer to be tucked up in bed right now.'

Halton continued muttering while he scratched his beard but Grant shrugged the comment off, instead returning to his assessment of the setup.

As he scanned the encampment two figures emerged from the tent and Leader joined them, handing over Grant's mobile phone. They exchanged a few words and then Leader came over and ordered Grant to get to his feet before handing over the phone. 'Call your office and tell them we want one million dollars for your release.'

'I already told you, I haven't got a million dollars. The company barely brings in a million pesos a month.'

'Then you must get it somewhere. Call your embassy, call your family, I don't care. The price is one million dollars.'

Grant toyed with his phone, weighing up his options. Just one look at the other prisoners told him this wasn't a situation he wanted to endure for any length of time, but he was telling the truth when he said his company didn't have that kind of money. He had about five hundred thousand dollars in his personal account, but to get access to that he would have to go through James Farrar, and he wondered briefly if decapitation would be a better alternative to another conversation with that snake. Sadly, he knew he had little alternative and he thumbed through his call history and dialled the number.

'What?' Farrar snapped, unhappy at being woken at such an ungodly hour.

'I have a problem and I need access to my account,' Grant told him.

'What's wrong? Your bed warmer got a bun in the oven?'

'Farrar, for once I want you to stop being a sarcastic prick and listen. I am being held by Abu Sayyaf and I need all the money in the account, plus another half million dollars.'

There was silence as Farrar took in the news and it seemed an age before the reply came, exploding into Grant's ear.

'You really are the most incompetent shit I've ever had the misfortune to deal with.'

Grant allowed him that cheap shot. 'Will you get the money?'

'It isn't our policy to negotiate with terrorists,' was the frank reply.

'You don't have to negotiate, you just have to pay them,' Grant said menacingly through gritted teeth, his patience with Farrar exhausted. Leader sensed the call wasn't going well and grabbed the phone from Grant's hand.

'I am Bong Manalo. Who is this?'

'James Farrar.'

'Well, James Farrar, we want one million dollars for the safe release of Sam Grant. You have until the end of the day to agree to pay or we will deliver his head to you.'

Manalo killed the connection and pushed Grant back to the ground before striding back to the men standing at the entrance to the tent.

'Who're the guys he's talking to?' Grant asked, nodding towards the trio.

'The taller one's name is Zandro Calizo, but they call him Jonjon. He's the main man. The other one is his second-in-command, Abel Guzman. Neither of them speaks English, so Bong acts as an interpreter.'

As she spoke there were raised voices from the trio, with Bong and Jonjon shouting at each other and Abel trying to calm them both down. Grant caught the word '*sundalos*' a few times and got the gist of the conversation: keep your voices down or you'll bring the soldiers down on us.

Bong eventually backed down and stomped off in a huff, taking his frustration out on anyone who got close enough, but it seemed everyone knew to keep out of his way when he was in this kind of mood.

The packing up moved at double-quick time and when they were ready to move off the group of prisoners was told to get to their feet. It was only then that Grant saw them tethered to each other by the ankle in groups of three. One of the younger terrorists came over and released Eddie Halton, then used a fresh piece of twine to tie him to Grant, turning a bad day into a really shitty one.

They were lined up in their little groups and, flanked by eight guards, they moved off into the jungle, the mosquitoes taking their turn to heap misery on them.

'You know, your voice sounds familiar,' Vick said to the back of Grant's head. 'I've heard it somewhere before, I'm sure of it.'

'Yeah, that happens a lot,' Grant said, not happy that she'd brought it up. Farrar may have changed his name and looks, but the voice remained the same, the voice which had been broadcast worldwide a year earlier.

'People say I sound like the guy in that advert,' he offered.

'Which advert?'

'You know, the one for car insurance.'

He left her with that vague answer and concentrated on putting one foot in front of the other in time with Halton.

James Farrar put his phone back on the bedside table and tousled his hair, trying to shake off the remnants of the previous night's sleep. He hated Mondays as a rule, and to start one this way wasn't going to do anything to help his mood.

He'd met some ill-disciplined people in his time, he thought, as well as his fair share of imbeciles, yet Grant was the only one who fell into both categories. Only an idiot could get himself kidnapped four days before a mission, one that had been manufactured especially for him. Well, perhaps *manufactured* was the wrong word, but they had been awaiting an opportunity to get Grant out into the field and one had presented itself in the shape of a small-time arms dealer who was looking to provide weapons to terrorist cells in Pakistan.

Hakan Farli was a Turkish national who had spent a few years selling small arms in his country of birth but was now hoping to step up to the big time. In order to do so he had spread the word about the services he offered, but unfortunately for him he had spread it too far and showed up on the MI6 radar in Islamabad while meeting with suspected terrorists. A full background check was done and the data sent to London where it was disseminated to all the other security services, and within hours a copy had been sent to James Farrar who saw Farli as the perfect opportunity to send Grant out into the open.

The plan had been simple: Grant, who would now be accompanied by Len Smart and Sonny Baines, would be tasked with tailing Farli with a view to causing an 'accident'. However, they themselves would be tailed, and the terrorist cell Farli was going to meet would be informed of their mission. Several of Farrar's men would be on the ground to record the moment the cell took them out and that video would then be shown to the other surviving co-conspirators as proof that Tom Gray was once and for all dead.

Of the eight men who had helped Tom Gray carry out his terrorist act—there was no other word for it in Farrar's opinion—Colin Avery and Michael Fletcher had died in Abdul Mansour's attack and two had passed away in the subsequent eleven months.

Farrar had been telling the truth when he'd told Grant that Tristram Barker-Fink had died in Iraq, but what he hadn't shared was the fact that it was Farrar's team who had leaked the route Tris and his principal would be taking. After the IED had been planted at the roadside by the insurgents it came down to just waiting for their convoy to pass.

Paul Bennett had been involved in a tragic motorcycle accident while he was doing over eighty miles per hour on the motorway. No other vehicles were involved in the incident, but only a select few knew that the people in the car following him at the time worked for Farrar. A portable heat gun had been focused on the back wheel of the bike for just a few hundred yards, its beam intense enough to compromise the integrity of the tyre wall and cause the fatal blowout.

That left just Carl Levine, Jeff Campbell, Baines and Smart to eliminate. Oh, and of course Sam Grant, he reminded himself.

Farrar would have happily let Grant rot in the jungle for a couple of years, but there was growing pressure to tie up all the loose ends as soon as possible. Besides, there was an agreement in place to show a video of Grant to his friends, with new footage to be provided every fortnight, as proof that he was still alive and that the government were sticking to their side of the bargain. He could of course just inform the Abu Sayyaf leadership that the man they thought was Sam Grant was in fact a British agent, but selling his death at the hands of terrorists to his friends would be difficult and raise too many questions. What was he doing there? What was done to try and get him out? Well, they could hardly send in the SAS to rescue a man who should be dead, but ...

Stumbling upon the possibility of killing three birds with one stone he did a quick mental calculation that told him it was close to midnight in England. A bit late to be calling, he thought, but if he'd had his sleep disturbed, why not pay it forward? He picked up his phone and dialled the first number. It answered on the second ring. 'Hello?'

'Len, it's James. I need to tell you about a change in the contract.'

'You're not cancelling it, are you?'

'No, it has become a recovery mission, that's all I can tell you at the moment,' Farrar said, not needing to point out that it was an unsecured line. 'Tickets will be waiting at the KLM desk at Heathrow and you'll be met at the airport when you get here.'

'What's the terms?' Len Smart asked.

'Same daily rate as we discussed, plus five thousand on completion.'

'And the terrain; how should I pack?'

'It'll be mostly jungle,' Farrar said.

'I'll need some equipment when I get there.'

'I'll provide everything you need,' Farrar promised.

'Okay, see you tomorrow.'

That's how it should be done, Farrar thought. *No quibbling, no arguments, just get the instructions and be ready to move. If only Grant could be like that.* He ended the call and gave the same instructions to Sonny Baines, who also readily agreed. It was a shame they had to die, but when you dance with the devil . . .

His next call was to the office.

'It's me. I need you to track a mobile phone,' he said and read out the number. 'It should be somewhere in Mindanao. I want an exact fix and constant updates on its movement.'

With the wheels in motion he cranked the air conditioning up a notch and jumped into the shower to prepare for what he knew was going to be a long day.

Chapter Four

Monday 16 April 2012

'What do you know about our brothers in the Philippines?'

That had been the simple question, and Abdul Mansour had answered honestly: very little.

It had been asked at a meeting just over the Afghan border from his home in Pakistan and he had told them what he knew, which was that Abu Sayyaf had had some notable successes in the past, including the kidnapping for ransom of several foreign nationals, and of course the ferry bombing in 2004 which had killed over a hundred people. There had been other minor incidents in recent years but nothing that had made international headlines. Beyond that he knew little of their current strength or future strategy, and said as much.

'They are more concerned with internal and regional feuds than striking out against their oppressors,' Azhar Al-Asiri had told him. 'They need some proper leadership in order to focus their attention.'

Al-Asiri had long been both Osama Bin Laden's deputy and the brains behind Al-Qaeda but had nowhere near the charisma of the man he called the Sheikh. He had been happy to let the Amir front the organisation while secretly pulling the strings from behind the scenes. In fact, it was Al-Asiri who had suggested taking things to a global level. Bin Laden's initial fight had been against the presence of American soldiers on Saudi soil, but it was Al-Asiri who had planted the idea of aiding fellow Muslims in their grievances, wherever they may be. There had been financial support for Abu Sayyaf in the early days but that had dried up as their hierarchy had fragmented, splintering into separate groups.

'Our aim is to unify these pockets of resistance once more and turn them into a formidable ally, but we cannot do that with money and weapons alone. I would like you to go there and do for them what you have done for me here.'

'You will take them the weapons they need and show them how to use them. More importantly, you must get them to launch attacks against our enemies as soon as possible.'

Mansour hadn't questioned the need for an immediate strike. He'd simply accepted the mission without hesitation, honoured to have been chosen for such a task.

'You will not have long,' Al-Asiri told him. 'You will leave in seven days and I need you to return before the middle of May. I have a major offensive in mind and I want you to take part in the planning.'

Following Bin Laden's death the previous year Al-Asiri, in his early fifties, had taken over the reins, as had been widely anticipated by the western world. However, they were quick to dismiss him as a lamb to Bin Laden's lion, a sparrow to his eagle, and it pleased him that they had written him off so readily. So far he had done what his detractors had expected, which had been nothing whatsoever.

At least, so they thought.

His focus had been on building up an army of generals, men who would go into the world and train others so that one day they could launch a coordinated attack that would leave the infidels trembling at the mention of his name.

One such general was Abdul Mansour, whose rise through the ranks had been meteoric. From a humble British background he had quickly proven himself an excellent soldier, carrying out numerous raids against the occupying US and British forces in Afghanistan. His crowning moment, however, had been his attack on the stronghold of Tom Gray in England the previous year. The intention had been to prevent Gray revealing the location of a device set to kill thousands of people, and it had cost the lives of thirty young martyrs. The device had been found in time by the British authorities, but the audacity of the raid in such a short time had cemented his name in Al-Qaeda history. Mansour had come up with the idea himself and seventy-two hours after putting forward his proposal to the elders he was in the middle of the battle, taking several lives including that of Gray himself.

Upon his return to Pakistan he had received a hero's welcome and quickly been elevated up the ranks, going from foot soldier to tactician, from student to teacher. The recruits he trained were in awe of his achievements and he taught them that nothing was impossible if you trusted Allah with your life. Many men had passed through his hands, soaking up his courage and strength as well as his knowledge, and his exploits had come to the attention of the very highest in the organisation.

To his great regret, Mansour hadn't been able to meet Osama Bin Laden in person. A meeting had been arranged in Abbottabad but the US Navy Seals struck two days before Mansour could be introduced to his master. That had been a personal blow, but he'd soon found that Azhar Al-Asiri was a more than fitting replacement, and it was Al-Asiri who had been instrumental in his successive promotions.

Mansour began overseeing the training of all new recruits and Al-Asiri was impressed with the results. He was even more impressed with Abdul's suggestion of a series of coordinated strikes around the world, something which fitted his global ambitions, and had considered it for many weeks before convening a meeting between the highest ranks of the organisation. The idea was discussed and agreed upon, with generals dispatched to a variety of countries to make their preparations.

Azhar Al-Asiri had personally chosen Abdul for what he considered the toughest assignment, which was why Mansour was now sitting on the rain-soaked deck of a *banca* heading for the island of Jolo, alongside his companion Nabil.

Nabil Shah was Mansour's lieutenant, an excellent soldier in his own right and a good friend over the last few years. Although older than Mansour, Shah had no qualms about taking orders from his general, a man who had proven himself in battle time and time again. Indeed, he thought it a privilege to serve him.

The journey had been long and arduous, beginning with a four-hundred-mile drive from Quetta south to the port of Karachi. It had taken a full ten hours to reach their first destination, travelling not only on main roads but also on rough tracks which often limited the speed to a mere ten miles an hour. At the port, they had been whisked aboard a freighter and given a cramped cabin for the seventeen-day trip. On nearing the port of Zamboanga Abdul, Nabil and their cargo had been transferred onto this vessel for the final leg of the journey. The boat looked like any other *banca* but boasted two giant Tohatsu outboard motors which could be swung into place at a moment's notice, making it easily capable of outrunning the local navy patrols. In addition, there was a box of shoulder-launched missiles on board which would discourage, if not sink, any of the Hamilton Class cutters that might manage to get in too close.

A lesser person might have taken the easier route of either flying to their destination or travelling most of the way overland, but Mansour was not only highly regarded within his own organisation; he was also known and sought throughout the world. Crossing just one border was a huge risk, so he had no hesitation in taking such a circuitous route. He'd filled his time using his 3G tablet PC to read up on Abu Sayyaf and their exploits over the years, using both the Internet and files provided by Al-Asiri.

Known to everyone else as Abu Sayyaf—meaning 'bearer of the sword'—they called themselves Al-Harakat Al-Islamiyya, 'Islamic Movement' and had been founded in the early nineties when they split from the Moro National Liberation Front (MNLF). Their first leader was Abdurajak Janjalani, a veteran of the fight against the Soviet occupation in Afghanistan, and their first major attack claimed the lives of two American evangelists in 1991. Shortly afterwards they claimed responsibility for the bombing of M/V Doulos, a Christian missionary ship docked in Zamboanga City Port.

Their attacks weren't limited to foreign nationals, as the Ipil raid in April 1995 proved. Desperate for funds, they had attacked the predominantly Christian town of Ipil in Zamboanga Del Sur, looting shops and banks while firing indiscriminately at civilians. Fifty-three people were killed in the attack and upwards of thirty—mostly women and children—were taken hostage as they retreated.

Another attack in 1999 had claimed the lives of six Christians when their jeep was attacked. Some of the victims were shot while others were hacked to death with *bolos*.

In the last decade their favoured method of attack, however, was bombings. From 2002 they had hit populated locations with the intention of causing as many casualties as possible. Targets included a karaoke bar in Zamboanga (killing three, including an American soldier), as well as a FitMart store in General Santos City where they killed fifteen.

In 2003 twenty-one people died when a waiting shed at the front of Davao airport was blown up, and on Valentine's Day 2005 they hit separate targets in General Santos City, Makati and Davao City, where they claimed eight lives.

Recent attacks had been sporadic, with only the attack on Tubigan village in Maluso, Basilan making international news. Eleven people died that day as up to seventy members of Abu Sayyaf raked houses with gunfire and set them ablaze in the pre-dawn raid.

In order to carry out these attacks, Abu Sayyaf needed weapons, and weapons cost money. In the early days they received funding through Mohammad Jamal Khalifa, a brother-in-law of Osama Bin Laden. Bin Laden had been a colleague of Janjalani during their Afghan Mujiheddin days and had provided his personal financial support until 1995 when Khalifa's connection to Abu Sayyaf was uncovered.

Having cut their ties with MNLF and by association the Malaysian group Jemaah Islamiyah in 1991, they had fore-gone their access to the major Al-Qaeda funding that had been channelled into the region, so they stepped up their kidnapping campaign as a way of supporting themselves. They had taken hostages in 1993 and 1996 (the latter managing to escape after thirteen days) but kicked it up a gear at the start of the next decade following the death of Abdurajak Janjalani. Instead of retaining his ideological focus they fell into kidnapping, murder and extortion in a big way under the rule of Janjalani's younger brother, Khadaffy.

There were four separate abductions in 2000, starting with several teachers and students from two schools in Tumahubong, Basilan. Father Rhoel Gallardo and three of the teachers were found murdered in May that year, the bodies showing indications of torture. Following that was the Sipadan kidnapping in which twenty-one people were taken from a dive resort in Malaysia, with most of them being released within a few months. During that time TV evangelist Wilde Almeda and some of his Jesus Miracle Crusade 'prayer warriors' turned up at the Abu Sayyaf camp in Jolo, Sulu, to pray for the hostages. Unfortunately, they themselves became captives and were held until being rescued by the military nearly four months later.

American Jeffrey Schilling became a hostage under totally different circumstances in August 2000, reportedly walking into their camp following an invitation from one of the Abu Sayyaf members who was related to his wife. Abu Sayyaf demanded a ransom of ten million US dollars but he managed to escape and was picked up by a local military patrol in April the following year.

In 2001 one of the highest profile kidnappings took place when twenty foreign nationals were grabbed from tourist resort Dos Palmos Beach in Palawan, including three Americans: Martin and Gracia Burnham, and Guillermo Sobero. A fortnight later a request was made for a Malaysian intermediary to negotiate a ransom payment but instead they came under attack from AFP soldiers. After they managed to evade the soldiers, Sobero was taken into the jungle and beheaded, a move designed to show that Abu Sayyaf were taking the situation seriously, even if the Philippine government were not.

It was over a year later that Martin Burnham and Ebidorah Yap, a Filipino nurse, were killed when the AFP launched yet another attack. Martin's wife Gracia was wounded in the leg but survived, and a subsequent investigation showed that it was AFP bullets which had been to blame for all three casualties.

Following the botched rescue the US Army sent six hundred military advisors as part of Operation Freedom Eagle (later to come under the Enduring Freedom umbrella). In addition the CIA sent elite paramilitary officers of the Special Activities Division (SAD). As a result, kidnappings fell to an all-time low, but not before they abducted six Jehovah's Witnesses and their Muslim guides in 2002. Two of the preachers were beheaded and some of the captives managed to escape before the rest were rescued by government troops in May 2003.

Khadaffy Janjalani himself was killed in action in 2006 and in 2007 Jainal Antel Sali Jr, known to all as Abu Sulaiman and Khadaffy's likely successor, was killed by the AFP.

Mansour had soaked all of this information up during his journey, and his conclusion was that the kidnappings had probably tailed off because of the relentless pressure being applied by the US and Philippine forces, as well as a lack of continuous leadership.

No matter, he thought, as he saw the island of Jolo appear on the distant horizon. Their days of limited funds would soon be over thanks in no small part to the cash he was bringing, as well as the promise of continued financial support for years to come.

The man he was due to meet was called Abu Assaf, the current head of the Abu Sayyaf organisation. Mansour had very little information about the man, except that he was in his forties and had stepped into the vacant position after the previous leader was shot by a raiding party led by a US SAD team four months earlier. He was glad that he was going into the initial meeting with no preconceptions; he preferred to form his own opinions based on what he experienced, not what he had heard from others.

'It has been a long journey,' Nabil said, gazing out towards the horizon.

'Our journey is just beginning,' Mansour replied. 'Once we arrive it is imperative that we get them to strike as soon as possible. I will remain here while we plan the attack, but after that I will be moving on. I would like you to stay here and show them how to organise themselves against the infidels.'

Shah nodded, showing no emotion, though deep down he was proud to be offered the opportunity to prove himself again.

It was over an hour before they neared the shore. Unsurprisingly, it wasn't a commercial port they drew up to but simply a deserted beach. A group of men was waiting and as soon as the anchor went out they waded into the water and began unloading the boxes he had brought. One man was supervising the transfer and Mansour made a beeline for him.

'*Salam alaikum!*' the man said, and Mansour returned the greeting.

'I am Jun,' he said. 'We go soon.'

It was obvious to Mansour that he wasn't much of a conversationalist, and equally apparent that there were not enough men to carry all of the baggage he had brought. Jun saw this too, and ordered half of the consignment to be camouflaged and appointed two armed guards to watch over it. The rest of the boxes were picked up and Jun led the way into the jungle, with Mansour and Shah following in his footsteps.

The march to the camp was slow going, mainly due to the weight of the boxes but also because they were avoiding known tracks, instead relying on Jun to cut a way through the dense vegetation with his *bolo*. This turned out to be the most intense part of his journey, knowing that somewhere on this small island there were close to two hundred US and Filipino troops who would just love to get their hands on him, and here they were crawling along at a snail's pace.

They stopped twice on their way to the camp, the second time for over an hour as a patrol ventured close. They crouched in silence as the soldiers made camp just thirty yards away and started cooking up their lunch. Mansour could see a few of the Abu Sayyaf were itching to take them on but Jun threw them looks which warned them to just stay quiet. Eventually the patrol moved on and they were able to make the last mile and a half without further encounters.

It was hardly recognisable as a camp. The only distinguishing feature was the number of people gathered in the small clearing, with no permanent structures to suggest they would remain here for any length of time.

Abu Assaf came to greet them effusively, arms spread wide and a toothless smile on his face, then ushered them over to a log next to a small fire. Three large fish were cooking over the flames and a pot of rice bubbled away on a small gas stove. Mansour suddenly realised that he hadn't eaten in over twenty hours and graciously accepted the invitation to dine.

'I understand you have gifts for us,' Assaf said in excellent English, the accent British.

Mansour nodded and led him over to the boxes arranged at the centre of the clearing. The first one he opened was the size of a family suitcase and contained nothing but cash, over two million American dollars in twenties and fifties, and Mansour was glad to note that Assaf's reaction was muted appreciation. There were no signs of greed on the man's face, just a look that said 'this could come in handy.'

The next box to be opened revealed dozens of brand new M16 rifles still wrapped in protective wax paper. 'Rather than AK-47s, we decided to provide weapons your enemies use because this way you can make use of any captured ammunition,' Mansour said.

He gestured to a couple of boxes and explained that they were full of 5.56 mm rounds for the rifles, then opened the next container.

'Claymore mines,' he said, lifting one out to show it to Assaf. 'These will help with setting up defensive perimeters and discouraging your enemies from following you,' he explained when he saw the look of confusion.

He smiled as he pointed to the next three boxes. 'These will be the difference between a struggle with the AFP and driving them out of the land,' he said. Releasing the catches on one of the lids, he swung it open to reveal a Dillon Aero M134 mini-gun. The six-barrelled weapon fired 7.62 mm bullets at an astonishing fifty rounds per second, fed from a 4400-round magazine.

'In the other boxes I have grenades, C4 explosive, ammunition for the M134 and twenty single-shot RPG-27s. Bear in mind, this is just a down payment on the support we are willing to offer you.'

'What are you asking in return?' Assaf asked, clearly satisfied with the gifts.

Mansour placed an arm around his shoulder and led him away to a quiet spot at the edge of the clearing. 'We want only what you want: to drive the infidels from the land. To do that you must become a force to be reckoned with, and I will show you how. The days of cowering in the jungle will soon be over for Abu Sayyaf.'

'We do not cower,' Assaf said harshly, aggrieved at the suggestion.

'Perhaps not, but while the AFP and the Americans wander calmly through your towns, you are sleeping up here in the hills. That is the first thing we need to change.'

'How do we do that? There are barely a hundred of us.'

'Don't you have any men on the surrounding islands that you can call on?' Mansour asked.

'There are perhaps another hundred spread throughout the Sulu Sea, but they have hostages and are trying to negotiate their release.'

'Bring them all here,' Mansour said. 'You have no more need to risk the lives of your men for mere money; we can provide all you need.'

Assaf nodded, making a mental note to pass on the order while Mansour continued with the questions.

'When was the last time you launched an attack on the infidels?'

'Attack? We can barely defend ourselves, never mind launch an attack. Besides, there are American soldiers here—elite American soldiers.'

'Who have a strictly non-combatant role, as I understand,' Mansour smiled. 'Tell me everything you know about their base.'

'I know much about their base,' Assaf said, 'but attacking it would only cause them to double their efforts against us. It would be counterproductive.'

'Far from it, my friend. An attack on their base may indeed make them bring the fight to you, but it would also show Jemaah Islamiyah that Abu Sayyaf are no longer the poor relation they think you are. Your Indonesian brothers will sit up and take notice of you once again, and by reuniting with them the Muslim movement within the region will become stronger than you could ever imagine.'

'They will not join with us. They refuse to even talk to us, so how will this one attack change their mind?'

'It is quite simple,' Mansour said. 'I will act as your emissary to explain that they can join us and share the glory—as well as the support we will provide—or they can fend for themselves and we will no longer provide them with training, weapons or funds.'

'They are proud people,' Assaf argued. 'They will not submit to threats and intimidation.'

'As are we all, brother, but any man who puts his own pride before the will of Allah is not worthy of calling himself a true believer. I will give them one chance, and one chance only. Naturally, I shall be very diplomatic in my approach.'

Mansour could see that Assaf was still not convinced, but he was confident in his own ability to bring the two groups together.

'Let me worry about Jemaah Islamiyah, brother. All you need to do is help me plan the attack on their camp.'

Chapter Five

Monday 16 April 2012

Sam Grant found the going hard enough without having to keep step with Halton, whose bare feet were constantly slipping on the wet jungle floor. A rain shower had hit an hour earlier and the remnants were still falling from the dense canopy above, even though the clouds had long since gone. While it cooled him down and provided some much-needed drinking water, it also turned the floor to gloop which his trainers were struggling to cope with, despite the decent tread on the sole. The camber of the route they were taking didn't help, either, and the undulating terrain meant they were either climbing or descending, rarely walking on level ground.

Things got much worse when they came to a river and Bong signalled for everyone to break for food. Most made their way to the bank and took in as much water as they could, while Vick and Moore waded into the water to give themselves a quick wash. They did so without removing any garments, and Grant guessed this was due to shyness on their part. Once they'd finished they sat down next to Grant and Halton.

'It's really hard washing yourself with all your clothes on,' she said. 'I nearly got a beating the first time I stripped down to my bra and panties. I haven't taken these off since,' she said, fingering the ragged material of the khaki blouse. 'Apparently it makes the Muslim men uncomfortable or something.'

'What's your story, Sam Grant?' asked Moore.

Before he could answer, Ox came and stood in front of him and rattled off some Tagalog that Grant barely understood, although he did catch the word '*sapatos*'—shoes. Feigning ignorance, Grant simply shrugged but it wasn't enough to deter Ox, who grabbed one of his feet and hoisted it into the air.

'Akin 'to,' Ox said. *These are mine.*

Rather than get into a confrontation Grant slipped off his sneakers and handed them over. Ox snatched them and walked off to try them on, leaving Grant with not so much as a '*salamat*'.

'You'll get used to that,' Halton said. 'What's yours is theirs, period. You'll be lucky to hold on to that T-shirt for much longer.'

Sure enough, Ox was back moments later. He whipped off his grimy *sando* and threw it at Grant, holding out his hand for the Lacoste T-shirt in exchange. Again, Grant handed it over without complaint and Ox trotted away to show off his new attire. Grant considered ditching the stinking rag but knew he would be grateful for it when the mosquitoes got into full attack mode. He did, however, start to imagine the things he would do to Ox should the chance present itself.

'So?' Vick asked.

'So what?' Grant replied, confused.

'What's your story?'

'Oh yeah, sorry. My mind was elsewhere.' He told them about the death of Alma's brother and his abduction from the hotel, and when asked for his reason for being in Manila he gave them the same story he'd told his girlfriend when they had met. Throughout the monologue he was acutely aware of Vick staring at him, a look of fierce concentration on her face. When he finished he stared back at her and she blushed when she realised what she had been doing.

'I'm sorry, but you just look so familiar,' she explained.

'There's an exhibit in the British Museum called Neanderthal Man. Maybe you saw me there.'

She shrugged off his weak joke and the look of concentration returned, and Grant was thankful when their dinner was served: a pile of rice on a large leaf. Everyone tucked in, grabbing handfuls of the bland food and shoving it in their mouths as fast as they could manage. It was a free-for-all, with plenty of shoving and pushing, and the leaf was picked clean within a couple of minutes. Grant had managed to get one decent handful and could have easily outmuscled the others to get more, but their condition was much worse than his and he figured they needed the nutrition more. If he was going to be here any length of time he would have taken all he could, but he was determined not to be in it for the long haul. Either Farrar would come up with the money, or he'd fight his way out.

Halton suddenly reached down to his ankle and began undoing the twine.

'What are you doing?' Grant asked, worried that his companion was about to do something stupid.

Halton shouted 'Ebbs ako,' and the nearest guard looked at him and nodded his head.

'I'm going to park my breakfast,' he told Grant, and wandered away from the group grabbing a couple of large leaves on the way.

'They just let you wander off on your own?' Grant asked, clearly surprised. 'Aren't they worried that you'll run off?'

'You have to stay in view,' Vick explained. 'If you disappear into the jungle they'll come after you with their *bolos*. You don't want that to happen, trust me.'

Grant assured her he would do no such thing. 'You've heard my story. What about you?' he asked.

'I'm a travel writer,' she said. 'I was doing a story about Apulit Island in Palawan and was enjoying an evening on Rob's boat. He has a charter company on the island and a few of us were on the sunset cruise when they struck.'

'How many others were there?' Grant asked.

'There were seven of us in all: Rob and I plus five Filipinos. They transferred us onto their boat and brought us here.'

'Are the others here?'

He could see the pain in her eyes when he asked the question, and suddenly wished he hadn't.

'There were two couples and one of them had a daughter, Carmen. She was only three ...' Her voice tailed off as the tears came, and Grant guessed this wasn't the first time she had cried since being here.

'They threw Carmen overboard on the second day,' Moore explained, putting an arm around Vick's shoulder and cradling her head against his chest. 'She had been crying, probably because she was so hungry, and when her mother couldn't settle her down one of them just grabbed her and tossed her over the side like she was a bag of rubbish.'

'Christ!' Grant said, astonished that anyone could be so deliberately brutal towards a child.

'The mother dived straight in after her,' Moore continued. 'Before they could stop him, the father jumped, too. We were about halfway through our journey at the time, which meant they were about a hundred and fifty miles from land.'

He didn't need to elaborate for Grant to understand what he was trying to say: there was no way they could have survived.

'The other two made it here with us, but after ten days the husband was taken for a walk and never came back. When the wife couldn't arrange her ransom she was taken for a walk, too.'

'What about Eddie?' Grant asked, nodding in the direction of the squatting figure ten yards away.

'He's just a tourist, and a pain-in-the-arse one at that,' Moore said. 'We all know the future doesn't look rosy but he bitches about it all day long. You'll learn to tune him out after a few weeks.'

'I hope it isn't going to take that long,' Grant said. 'Do they honour the ransoms that are paid?'

'Yes, so far. There was a German guy here last month and he managed to arrange his ransom within a few days. He even sent a food package for us a week later, but all we got from it was a note. Bong had the rest.'

'Bong's English is good,' Grant noted.

'He was educated at De La Salle, the best university in Manila,' Vick said, having regained her composure. 'Comes from a well-off family who kicked him out of the house when they heard he was hanging out with Muslim friends, and he came down here to teach them a lesson. His friends introduced him to Jonjon and he signed up there and then.'

'Did he tell you this?'

'God no, it was Dindo,' she said, lowering her voice and gesturing towards one of the younger captors. 'He drops by every night and slips me some food when the others are asleep. I think he has a crush on me.'

Grant wasn't surprised, given her looks. 'Bong doesn't seem very friendly. Are they all like that?'

'To be honest, most of them treat us as well as can be expected. Bong is the exception, though. I think there's a little power struggle going on there.'

'How so?'

'He's told us on more than one occasion that we are being treated too well, and that when he takes command things will become a lot tougher for us. I think the conflict stems from their goals. While Bong is fighting for an independent Muslim state, Dindo thinks Jonjon and Abel are in it for the money, pure and simple.'

Grant glanced upstream where the senior Abu Sayyaf members were gathered and the power struggle became a little more even as a plume of red erupted from Jonjon's chest, spraying blood all over Guzman's head and neck. The report from the bullet followed a millisecond later.

'*Sundalos!*'

As the shout went up, their captors grabbed their weapons and began returning fire, spraying bullets into the undergrowth in the general direction of the initial round on the far bank of the river. As bullets began peppering the area, Vick and the rest of the hostages tried to make themselves as small as possible but Grant knew it was just a matter of time before one of them was hit. He sought a defilade position and saw one a few yards away, a slight depression behind the rotting trunk of a fallen tree. He grabbed Vick and began pulling her towards it, then remembered that she was still attached to Moore.

'Move!' he shouted at them, but Moore had frozen, his body shutting down in response to the assault. Grant leaned over Vick and grabbed him by the ear, twisting it as hard as possible. Moore had no option but to follow, and Grant pulled them to the safety of cover.

The fire intensified on both sides, and Grant realised that Bong's warning about the AFP was true: they were more likely to kill the hostages than rescue them. Fire from both sides was indiscriminate, and Grant wondered how many of the AFP had their eyes opened during the attack. Bullets strafed the log and a cry went out as one of the Filipino hostages took a round to the calf, a round that would have done serious damage to Vick or Moore if he hadn't dragged them to safety.

Grant gauged the incoming fire and estimated that there were five or six attackers at best, suggesting a small recon patrol, an extremely stupid recon patrol, given the circumstances. In their position he would have laid up and called in reinforcements rather than try to take on a much larger force, especially one holding hostages.

One of the guards went down with a wound to the throat but he was ignored by his compatriots as they continued to repel the attackers. A couple of grenades were lobbed across the narrow river, one landing harmlessly short but the other bouncing its way into the vegetation, taking out two AFP soldiers.

Grant nearly jumped with fright when a body landed next to him and he turned to see Halton cowering by his side, trousers still around his ankles.

'Unbe-fucking-lievable! Whose side are they on, for Christ's sake?'

Grant ignored him, instead concentrating on one of the Abu Sayyaf who had picked up the loaded RPG. His stance was all wrong, and as he fired he lost his balance, falling flat on his backside. Luckily for all concerned—except the AFP—the explosive head went where he had aimed.

Crump.

A tree took the brunt of the impact, cracking the trunk in two, but the AFP got the message and their attack petered out as they retreated back through the jungle, firing sporadically as they ran.

With the battle having lasted barely more than a couple of minutes a sense of calm returned to the jungle, but the Abu Sayyaf members were still pumped up, keeping a close watch on the far bank. The silence didn't last long, however, as the Filipino woman who'd been hit in the leg began to make the transition from shock to pain. Her cries were ignored by the guards, who were more intent on dealing with their own fallen, two of whom were clearly dead. The other casualty was one of the younger Abu Sayyaf who had sustained a flesh wound to the arm, and he showed it off proudly, pleased with his new battle scar.

Bong began barking orders and the two bodies were wrapped in hammocks, ready to be carried away. Others were instructed to see to the hostages and they began by ensuring everyone was tethered to at least one other person. When they got to the injured woman they seemed at a loss as to what to do. Her screams were intensifying all the time and any attempts to treat the wound simply increased her hysteria.

After a couple of minutes Bong purposefully strode over to them and surveyed the situation. It was clear to everyone that the woman was not going to be able to walk on the injured leg, and the noise she was making would only serve to alert the AFP as to their whereabouts. He rattled off more orders in Tagalog and the tether was removed from the woman's other ankle.

Grant watched the proceedings but had no idea what was being said, the words spitting out like automatic weapon fire. Bong gestured with his arm and the hostage who had been cradling the casualty was suddenly dragged away, and his own screams began to drown out those of the woman Grant assumed to be his wife or girlfriend. He was kicking and screaming as they pulled him clear, and Grant suddenly knew what was coming. He grabbed Vick and cradled her head into his chest just as Bong lowered his rifle and ended the woman's pain with a single shot to the head. Her partner collapsed in tears, howling with grief, and Bong was clearly not in the mood to put up with it. He pointed the rifle at the man and barked out more instructions, but the heartbroken hostage either wasn't listening or didn't care. His cries continued for a moment as he stared at his loved one, then stopped as rage moved to the top of the emotional table. His face contorted and he clambered to his feet, anger etched on his face. Bong shouted at him to back off and raised his rifle to reinforce the threat, but the man kept coming, fists clenching as he approached. Another warning, but the advance continued, the man cursing venomously as he moved nearer.

'Bahala Ka!' *Suit yourself.*

The rifle spat one more time and the man collapsed in mid-stride. Abel Guzman came over and began remonstrating with Bong, who stood his ground and argued back, vehemently defending his actions. Everyone stopped what they were doing to watch the confrontation, which escalated when Guzman pushed Bong in the chest and he stumbled backwards, losing his footing on a tree root and splashing into the river. Apoplectic, he jumped up and ran for Abel, grabbing him round the throat and pinning him to a tree. Guzman tried to prise him off but Bong had too firm a grip, so he fumbled for a weapon as his face began to turn scarlet. He reached towards his *bolo* but Bong swung a knee up, deflecting his hand away from the handle of the knife. With his last remaining strength he tried to claw at Bong's face but his reach was half an inch short and his life ebbed away moments later.

Bong let him drop and spat on the corpse before cursing in deep, deep Tagalog. He turned and looked at his men, daring any to challenge him for the leadership, but none seemed in the mood, even though they were brandishing weapons.

Their tacit approval accepted, he gave orders to pack up while he himself took the cell phones from the fallen leaders and claimed their tent as his own.

Grant was once again tied to Halton, and was thankful that his companion had managed to dress himself once more, though his sarcasm hadn't deserted him. 'Just another day in paradise.'

'And it's about to get a lot worse with Bong in charge,' Moore said. He turned to Grant. 'Thanks. If you hadn't moved me, I'd hate to think what would have happened.'

'Don't mention it. Just make sure you take cover next time the bullets start flying.'

'That wasn't your first time in a gunfight, was it?' Vick asked.

'What do you mean?' Grant replied, but he was already aware of what she was implying. When the firefight had started, all of the hostages—and a couple of their captors—had frozen, dropping where they were. He had been the only one to seek protection. His army training had kicked in once more and while it may have saved his life again it was beginning to get noticed. If Vick and Robert could spot it, it wouldn't be long before one of the guards did, and that would make him dangerous in their eyes.

'I mean you knew how to react when they started shooting at us.'

'Self-preservation, I guess,' Grant shrugged, trying to play down the incident, but Vick wasn't ready to accept such a weak response.

'If it was self-preservation, why didn't you just look after yourself? Why did you drag Rob and me behind the tree?'

'I suppose I wasn't really thinking straight,' he said, knowing it wasn't far from the truth. Thankfully her questions stopped when they were ordered to get up and prepare to move out.

Lined up in pairs, they were given the bodies of the dead to carry and the formation moved off once more. Grant had the feet end of the hammock over his right shoulder and Eddie Moore, walking in front of him alongside Vick, carried the head end. For a man who had been used to carrying sixty-pound packs into battle it was still a bit of a struggle for Grant, especially in his stocking feet, but Moore was in shit state already without having this additional burden literally thrown on his shoulder.

Twenty minutes into the march, Moore had already stopped twice for a short rest and to change his grip, and Bong wasn't best pleased at the pace being set. He told one of his subordinates to take over on point and came back down the line to see what was causing the hold-up.

'Pick it up!' he shouted at Moore, who had dropped his end of the hammock so that he could massage his shoulder.

Grant laid his end on the ground and told Bong to let him have a rest. 'Can't you see he's in no condition to carry this kind of weight?'

Bong advanced towards him menacingly, despite the height disadvantage. Grant, having learned a lesson less than half an hour earlier, adopted a submissive posture rather than standing up to the man. It didn't prevent him getting a whack on the back with the flat edge of a *bolo*, but it helped to keep up the pretence.

Bong was readying himself to deliver another blow when one of the phones in his pocket chirped.

He dug it out and stabbed the 'Connect' button.

'Ano?' *What?*

He spoke for a couple of minutes, then ended the call with a simple 'Sige.' *Okay.*

'We are taking a boat ride,' he announced to the prisoners, and after a brief scan round to get his bearings he resumed point duty, leading them downhill towards sea level.

'Do they often move you from island to island?' Grant asked Moore as they once again picked up their load.

'No, we've always been here.'

Grant considered the implications. The AFP were on this island, which meant that if he could get away from the Abu Sayyaf he would have someone he could turn to. The next island, wherever it may be, might not contain any friendly forces at all, which meant escape would need to entail slipping away from his captors *and* stealing a boat *and* crossing an ocean. If he was going to end this any time soon, he would have to do it before they were loaded onto the boat.

Through a gap in the trees he saw the Sulu Sea in the distance and estimated that it would be a couple of days at their current pace before they reached the coast. Not much time, but it was all the time he had to come up with a plan.

James Farrar toyed with the phone as he considered the best way to word his message to Grant. When he called the cell phone he was certain it would be answered by one of the Abu Sayyaf, so he would demand to speak to Grant to make sure he was still alive and well. Two things that bothered him were that the message would have to be concise, and that their conversation might be on speakerphone.

The message he wanted to get across was that no money was going to be paid and that Baines and Smart were on their way to get him out, but how to say that in a way that only Grant would understand? He got up and made himself a cup of coffee, all the time trying to formulate a couple of short sentences that would carry the message.

It was almost an hour later that he picked up the phone and dialled Grant's number.

'It's James Farrar,' he said as soon as the connection was made. 'I want to speak to Sam.'

'Do you have the money?' Bong asked.

'We're putting it together but it will take a few days. In the meantime I want to speak to Sam. I want to be sure he's still alive.'

A moment later he heard Grant's voice. 'James, have you—'

Bong snatched the phone away. 'You have heard his voice. Call me in three days to arrange the transfer.'

'I want to speak to him, let him know that everything is okay.'

There was silence for a moment. 'You give me the message, I will pass it on,' Bong said.

Farrar had expected as much. 'Can't you just put me on speakerphone? He must be terrified and will want to hear a friendly voice.'

He heard mumbling as Bong tried to find the setting on the unfamiliar phone, but eventually he was instructed to relay his message.

'Sam, it's James. I hope you're bearing up under the pressure. I have asked a specialist company to handle the transfer. They are called Baines and Smart and they deal with hostage situations all the time, so I thought it best to let them do things their way. It might be a little expensive but I'm sure you understand.'

'Yes, James, I understand.'

Bong took the phone off speaker. 'You have passed on your message,' he said. 'Call me in three days with the arrangements.'

'Wait, I have instructions from Baines and Smart. They want me to call every eight hours to ensure he is still alive.'

'No,' was the simple reply.

'Then they won't make the transfer,' Farrar said. 'I'm not about to send more people in there so you can take them hostage, too. Either you let Baines and Smart handle it and follow their instructions, or the deal is off and you get nothing.'

Farrar held the phone to his ear, praying the bluff wasn't called, and the interminable silence was eventually broken. 'I will call you once a day at three o'clock in the afternoon.'

The phone went dead in his hands and Farrar realised he'd been holding his breath waiting for the response. Exhaling loudly, he went to the kitchen, uncorked a bottle of red wine and grabbed a glass, then settled on the sofa.

So, Grant's phone would be active every day at three in the afternoon, which should give Baines and Smart the opportunity to pinpoint his location, and hopefully Grant got the message that help was on its way; the last thing he wanted was the sonofabitch ruining his plan by escaping before the others arrived. There was always the chance that the man holding the phone might split off from the others but there was nothing he could do about that, and he wasn't one for worrying about things beyond his control.

After polishing off half of the wine he headed for bed, making a mental note of the equipment he would need to source in the morning. They would need weapons, a device to track him with, and some form of communications, both for the mission and to report in to him. Happy in the knowledge that he could have everything he needed delivered to the office he set the alarm for five and climbed into bed.

Grant pondered the message Farrar had sent him and kept coming back to the same conclusion: Sonny and Len were going to attempt a rescue mission.

While it was good news in one respect, he would have much preferred Farrar to stump up the cash. His friends were more than capable of pulling it off, especially if he was able to assist them somehow, but there was always the chance of a hostage or two getting hit in the melee. Paying the ransom was by far the best option, and the money could always be replaced, probably within a year the way the company was performing.

He pushed the thought aside. Focus, he told himself. Sonny and Len were probably already on their way, which meant they would be arriving in the Philippines in the next twenty-four hours. Adding time for a briefing and the trip down to Basilan, he reckoned they could be on the island by Wednesday morning. Unfortunately he and the others would reach the shoreline at roughly the same time, which meant his friends would end up scouring the wrong island for him.

He gave himself two priorities, the first of which was to slow their progress somehow. The second was to get his hands on a weapon.

Chapter Six

Tuesday 17 April 2012

Simon 'Sonny' Baines was shaken awake as turbulence tossed the Boeing 777-200 violently around the skies. Next to him, Len Smart was reading a detective mystery on his Kindle, oblivious to the chaos around him. It wasn't until an overhead locker broke open and disgorged its contents into the aisle that he tore himself away from the gripping story.

His watch told him that they were still six hours from Manila, having left Amsterdam's Schiphol airport an eternity earlier. The flight from Heathrow had been a short hop and after a three-hour stopover they had climbed aboard. An hour into the flight they'd had breakfast, which Sonny topped off with a scotch before falling into a deep sleep. Smart envied him the ability to sleep on planes, something he had never been able to master. A freezing hillside in the middle of winter was no problem, but not an airplane seat. It didn't matter if it was a civilian airliner or a military transport, he just couldn't nod off, no matter how tired he was.

'Do you think Tom will be joining us on the pickup?' he asked Sonny.

'He's got a new name now,' his friend reminded him in a low voice.

'Yeah, right. It's hard to get used to the idea after knowing him as Tom for ten years. I wonder what name he's chosen.'

'I guess we'll find out soon enough. What are you reading?'

'*Black Beast* by R. S. Guthrie.'

'Any good?'

'Brilliant,' Smart said, and promptly turned his attention back to the Kindle. Sonny shoved a pair of headphones over his ears and scanned the channels on the in-flight entertainment console, settling for an episode of Mr Bean, but as the plane cruised over central Asia he quickly lost all interest in the show. Instead he recalled the last time he had seen Tom. It had been in the ruins of the old pottery factory that had been transformed from fortress to rubble in an instant during the attack by Abdul Mansour and his men. Tom's plan to reform the justice system had been audacious, and had almost succeeded. It also nearly cost him his life.

It would be good to see his old friend again, Sonny thought, and closed his eyes to sleep away the rest of the flight.

It seemed just moments later when Len woke him. 'We'll be landing in fifteen minutes,' Smart said, stowing his Kindle in his rucksack. Sonny paid a quick visit to the toilet and then stopped by the galley to chat up the stewardesses. Despite being in his mid-thirties he looked ten years younger, and hadn't seemed to age a day since joining the SAS as one of their youngest recruits. The name Sonny soon stuck, and he used his boyish good looks at every available opportunity, with varying degrees of success. On this occasion he struck out and resumed his seat, staring out of the window as they approached Ninoy Aquino International Airport. After touching down they made their way through immigration and picked up their luggage, a suitcase each packed with items most of which they were never likely to use. It was just easier to throw some jeans and T-shirts into a case than explain why they were arriving for a holiday without a change of clothes.

As promised they were met at the exit. A Filipino in a white shirt and black trousers held up a card with their names as they fought through the crowd of taxi drivers looking for a chance to charge unsuspecting foreigners ten times the normal fare. Len and Sonny introduced themselves and were led out into the sunshine, and the first thing that hit them was the smell, an odour which seemed to be a combination of sewage and rotting food. As they walked to the pickup area the heat added to their woes, and they were thankful when they climbed into the air-conditioned SUV.

It took close to an hour to get the three miles to their destination, near the British Embassy in Makati. Manila has some of the most congested roads in the world, despite government efforts to keep the traffic flowing. Vehicle number plates end with a number, and each day two of those numbers were banned from the road. Despite this measure, journeys were most often made at a steady crawl at best. Along the way they had to contend with a variety of ancient trucks, buses and cars, and now and again they would spot a brand new vehicle that seemed very out of place. At each set of traffic lights their transport was assaulted by vendors or beggars, often seven-year-old girls carrying a baby and dressed in rags, holding out a hand in the hope of a dollar or two.

The SUV pulled into an underground car park below a thirty-storey office block. The driver opened the door for them, then led them to an elevator which took them to the seventeenth floor. The door at the end of the corridor proclaimed the office to belong to Knight Logistics Management, and they were shown into the reception where a lady in her fifties asked them to take a seat. A few moments later a connecting door opened and Farrar ushered them into his office, pointing towards a sofa as he sat on the corner of his desk. They dumped their luggage and took a seat.

'Gentlemen, thank you for coming at such short notice,' he said. The pleasantries out of the way, he laid out the details of the mission. 'Sam Grant has been kidnapped by Abu Sayyaf, a Muslim terrorist group operating in the southern Philippine islands. I want you to get him out.'

'Who's Sam Grant?' Smart asked.

'Ah, sorry, I forgot you didn't know. Sam Grant is the name Tom Gray goes by these days.' He paused to let the news sink in, pleased to see that it had come as something of a shock. If they'd recognised the name it would surely mean they'd been in contact with him, something he'd strictly forbidden.

I guess that answers the question: 'Is Tom coming with us?' Len thought. 'How did he get kidnapped?' he asked.

'I don't know all the details,' Farrar admitted, 'but whatever happened, I'm beginning to wonder if he's up to the job he's been chosen for.'

'Tom still has what it takes,' Sonny said quickly. 'If he was kidnapped it was because he knew that trying to fight his way out was a waste of time, but he'll be working on an escape, I guarantee it.'

'Does he know we're coming?' Len asked, changing the subject in an attempt to defuse the tension creeping into the room.

Farrar shared the message he'd relayed the previous evening, and they agreed that in all likeliness, Tom knew a rescue was going to be attempted.

'You said you'd have some equipment for us,' Len said, and Farrar walked over to a closet and retrieved a long sports holdall. Inside they found two Heckler & Koch MP5SD suppressed sub-machine guns, a pair of Beretta M9 pistols and two American M4 Carbine rifles with under-slung M203 grenade launchers. In addition there were ammunition, night vision goggles, a smart phone and a communication set comprising throat microphone and earpiece.

'These comm units use 2048-bit encryption and flash-burst the messages, so they're very hard to intercept or decrypt.' Flash-bursting meant compressing the whole message into a tiny blob of data and sending it when the user finished talking, so rather than anyone being able to hear their real-time conversation, any eaves-droppers would simply hear a millisecond burst of static.

'The phone will give your current location as well as the location of Sam's phone.' He opened an application on the phone and they saw a map of the Philippines, with a green dot flashing over their current location in Manila and a red cross on one of the southern islands. The map lacked topography, showing just the land masses as brown to the sea's blue. A scale on the right-hand side of the screen showed the distance between the two locations.

'How up to date is Tom's location?' Len asked.

'Sam's location,' Farrar said, emphasising the new name, 'will be real-time just as long as his phone is turned on. Abu Sayyaf have agreed to call me at three in the afternoon each day, so we know it will be updated at least once every twenty-four hours.'

He used his thumb and forefinger to expand the image with the red cross and hit a symbol at the top of the screen, which showed a dot-to-dot red trail. 'These are Sam's movements since they first made contact with me. It looks like they traversed the high ground and are heading towards the coast.'

'Do we know the enemy strength? Numbers, weapons, anything at all?'

'Nothing whatsoever. You'll be going in blind with just a cross on a map as your guide. Is there a problem with that?'

Smart and Baines looked at each other and had the same thought: this was a clusterfuck waiting to happen.

'What is it with people's perception of the SAS?' Sonny asked. 'Why does everyone think we're invincible superheroes? We only get the job done because we do our homework and know what we're facing, not by jumping in with our eyes closed and nothing but a mean expression and a huge set of balls.'

There was no animosity in his voice. A touch of sarcasm, perhaps, but no animosity. Farrar, however, chose to take it completely the wrong way.

'I'm beginning to wonder if anyone from your beloved regiment is capable of conducting a real mission these days,' he said, eyes directed towards Sonny. 'In case you didn't know, I called you as soon as I found out that he'd been kidnapped. That was only twenty-eight hours ago, and considering we don't have any assets down there, and given the fact that I haven't been able to have a private conversation with him to get any first hand intel, it is impossible to know anything about what you will be facing. But then, you'd know that if you were smart.'

'He's Smart,' Sonny said, pointing to Len. 'I'm pragmatic, and this has nothing to do with being capable of conducting a real mission. This is about the seven Ps: Proper Prior Planning Prevents Piss Poor Performance.'

Len put a hand on his friend's arm to calm him down. 'We've been in worse situations,' he said to Sonny, then turned to Farrar. 'We'll do it, but the price just went up. Thirty thousand on completion. Each.'

'Twenty,' Farrar countered.

'Twenty-five.'

'Done. There's a plane waiting to fly you to Zamboanga but you'll have to make your own way from there. My driver will take you back to the airport and show you through the diplomatic channel so you'll avoid having to check in the bag. My secretary will provide you with the necessary passes.'

He stood and ushered them out of his office, handing Sonny the bag after they'd collected their own luggage, and as promised there were two name badges waiting for them on the secretary's desk, each complete with a recent photo.

'My number is programmed into that phone, which uses satellite rather than 3G, so you should have a signal wherever you are,' Farrar said. 'I'll keep you updated if there are any developments.'

The driver was waiting in the hallway to take them back to the car park.

'I would have done it for the original five grand,' Sonny said to Len as they walked towards the elevator.

'For Tom, I would have done it for nothing,' Len replied.

When he was alone in his office Farrar checked his watch and calculated the time it would take them to arrive on Basilan and make their way into the jungle. The ideal scenario was for them to be within sight of Grant before he gave their location away, but unless they fed him regular updates he doubted he would get to know when they were close enough. He decided to wait until Bong called him tomorrow for his three o'clock conversation with Grant and break the news then. He would then have the location and could guide them in to what would surely be an ambush.

It wasn't as if they were likely to manage a rescue in the meantime, not with the ammunition he'd supplied. Any soldier with as much time on the range as the SAS had would be able to tell if all of the explosive propellant had been removed from a bullet, so the powder in the rounds he'd given them had been replaced with plain old sand. Figuring that they would have no reason to fire their weapons until they got into a battle with Abu Sayyaf, he had no concerns about them discovering his little subterfuge until it was too late. The only thing that could scupper his plans was if they found Grant as soon as they landed on the island, but if the AFP and US special forces had trouble locating anyone from Abu Sayyaf, he was damn sure a couple of ex-soldiers—no matter how good they once were—would find it a struggle to locate them.

With Baines, Smart and Grant out of the way he could then turn his attention to the two remaining conspirators, Carl Levine and Jeff Campbell. They would demand some kind of explanation as to why their friends had disappeared, which was the reason he'd videotaped the conversation they'd just had. That would keep them quiet for a while, giving him the chance to put together a plan to eliminate them and close down the operation. After that he would finally be free to return home to England and be rid of this terrible climate once and for all.

He knew he would have to be quick, though, as having five friends die within a year would be seen as too much of a coincidence, especially when these five knew something that could cause serious embarrassment to the government. The deaths of Barker-Fink and Bennett would arouse little suspicion on their own, but when Baines and Smart disappeared along with Grant he was sure Campbell and Levine would begin asking questions. This made their demise all the more critical, so he went to his computer, entered his password to open the secure file and began reading up on the preparations for their deaths.

He knew that Campbell had booked a holiday in Florida for himself, his wife and his three children and would be leaving in nine days, so he was the priority target. The surveillance operation had noted a few of his most common habits, including the darts night at his local pub, The Wheatsheaf, every Wednesday evening. He also went jogging at seven o'clock every morning, and these two opportunities were the ones the team were currently working on. The last updates to his file were his UK team's three suggestions for the takedown. Dismissing the first two—a hit-and-run accident and a common pub fight—as too obvious and risky, he pondered the third option. They wanted to fake a burglary and kill him in the process. A man of his nature would surely try to defend his family, the team suggested, and they could kill him when he tried.

Farrar wasn't so sure. If Campbell didn't resist and just let them take his possessions, the team would have no reason to kill him. If they did kill him under those circumstances, his family would surely know that he was the real target and they would have to be silenced, too, which was something he didn't want to contemplate. Not yet, at least.

Adding a note to the team to come up with some other options by the end of the day, he closed Campbell's file and moved on to the next one.

Levine, too, was a creature of habit. Twice a week he went skydiving at the local airport and the team had managed to get one of their number into his Tuesday evening sessions. Like Levine, their man was an ex-paratrooper and through that common bond they had become friends over the last four weeks. Their report said he was now in a position to gain access to Levine's rig with a view to sabotaging it. Farrar didn't understand the intricacies of how they intended to rig the parachute, but they assured him that both the main and reserve would fail to operate on the last dive of the day. Their man would cry off that last jump, claiming to have a prior engagement, and as he had used a false name—belonging to a real ex-para he'd served with—and the licence plates on his car were also false, there was nothing but a description to link him to the death. Once he'd shaven off the full beard and had a haircut, the authorities would be searching for a ghost.

Farrar was satisfied with the plan and gave the go-ahead to implement it the following week.

Another few days, he thought, and he could finally get a proper roast beef dinner. For now, though, he had to be satisfied with a half-decent shepherd's pie from the local English pub.

Chapter Seven

Wednesday 18 April 2012

Sam Grant woke as yet another mosquito helped itself to a drink from his exposed arm. Instinctively he tried to swat it, and that was when he remembered the handcuffs. They had been produced as the sun fell the previous evening, and he had been shackled to a tree and left to sleep in a sitting position. When he asked what he was supposed to do if he needed the toilet he was simply told to hold it until the morning. With that, his vision of a night escape had vanished, leaving him with not only dented optimism but also a very full bladder.

When one of the guards stirred close by Grant called out to him.

'Ihi ako,' he said, letting the man know he was desperate for a piss.

The guard rubbed his eyes and then dug into his pocket for the keys, and as he ambled past Grant he dropped the key by the base of the tree and continued on to answer his own call of nature. After a little fumbling Grant managed to free himself and stood up on legs filled with pins and needles, a product of his awkward sleeping position. Still, he managed to move a few steps to the edge of the clearing and finally relieve himself. The thought occurred to him that he was losing a lot of fluid and not taking much in, and if he didn't change the ratio soon he was going to start feeling the effects.

However, that wasn't the most troubling thought rattling around in his head.

The previous evening, in line with Muslim tradition, the bodies of Jonjon and Abel were buried as soon as was practical. Grant and the others had been given the task of digging the grave while the Abu Sayyaf washed the dead and shrouded them in hammocks, these being the only white material they had.

With the bodies laid to rest, their heads pointing towards Mecca, the pace of the march had picked up considerably and the beach was no more than five hours away; they would reach it long before Sonny and Len could get into the area. His only hope was that they would lie up close to the shore and wait until nightfall before boarding the boat, but that was far from guaranteed.

Movement near his foot caught his eye and he saw a six-inch-long black millipede slink past his toes. He followed its path and watched it crawl inside a fallen tree trunk, where he noticed the particularly sharp remnants of a branch that had been snapped off, probably when it was felled. The stub of the branch gave him an idea, and he knew what he had to keep an eye out for.

He rejoined the group, most of whom were already awake and preparing for another day in the jungle. Halton in particular was in good voice.

'Who's Dina?' Vick asked, catching Grant totally off guard.

'What made you ask that?'

'You were saying the name over and over in your sleep,' she said. 'You must have been dreaming.'

Grant knew which dream she was referring to. It was one he had at least three times a week and it never varied. He is in the car with Dina driving and Daniel in the back seat, all three of them heading towards the beach for a mini break. He is enjoying the beautiful sunshine and Daniel's singing when the song suddenly stops and the sky darkens, thundery black clouds blotting out the sun. He looks in the back seat and Daniel is flopping from side to side, his eyes lifeless. He turns to tell Dina but she is removing her seatbelt, foot planted on the accelerator and their speed building with each passing second. He tries calling out to her, telling her not to do it, to stay with him, but her focus is on the approaching bridge spanning the motorway. He screams her name again and she is smiling now, not at him, but at the bridge support looming large. He tries to reach across to her but his own seatbelt is so tight that he can't move a muscle.

'DINA!'

With that final scream the dream ends, a split second before they crash headlong into the concrete pillar.

'Dina was someone I knew once,' he said. 'It was a long time ago.'

'The name's familiar,' she said, curiosity once more etched on her face.

'It's not that unusual. I went to school with three girls called Dina,' Grant lied. He could see Vick racking her brains for a glimmer of recollection but he wasn't about to help her. Instead he stood and did some stretches to try to eliminate some of the muscle knots he had accumulated during the night. In the distance he heard the sound of a light aircraft, and moments later his captors began shouting for everyone to move to cover. Grant followed everyone's lead and jogged into the trees. He squatted down, head up in search of the plane. It passed over a minute later, a single-engine Cessna T41-B.

'They fly over every few days,' Moore told him nervously.

'Yeah, and every time they fly over we get attacked a few hours later,' Halton added.

Grant ignored the morale officer's whining and considered how he could turn this to his advantage. In the undergrowth he searched around for something that could be used as a weapon and found the perfect item—a twig the thickness of his thumb with a point at one end where it had been cut from a tree. It even had a growth on either side, so his hand wouldn't slip down the shaft when he used it. He slipped the eight-inch shiv into his sock and pulled his pant leg over it for concealment, careful to make sure no-one noticed his movements.

Once the sound of the engines died away, Bong instructed everyone to get up and start packing away, seemingly desperate to leave the immediate area. Even though trees had been cut down to make the clearing, they were only the younger plants—the canopy overhead remained in place, just as it had in the other camps they had forged. Grant thought it unlikely that they would have been spotted from the air, but the others obviously had differing opinions and their eyes scanned the jungle as they stuffed possessions into their packs, weapons always close at hand.

Within ten minutes they were on the move again, and Grant tried to keep pace with Dindo while at the same time trying not to make it too obvious. It meant Halton had to move at the same speed, which did nothing for his demeanour.

Grant found it unnerving that now and again Vick would turn and look at him with a puzzled expression, and he wondered how close she was to guessing his true identity. Given the current situation it might not be that big a problem, he thought, especially if she didn't make it out of the jungle. However, if she managed to secure her release and shared the news with others, he knew Farrar would make him disappear again, but this time permanently.

After five hours they were within smelling distance of the sea and Grant thought his wish was going to come true when Bong ordered everyone to make camp. Through a gap in the trees he could see the beach about half a click away, a sheltered cove with a golden, sandy beach. He was thankful that there was no sign of a boat, adding to his hope that they would wait until dark to transfer to the next island.

As a fire was prepared and rice thrown into a pot he realised how hungry he was, but was more intent on scanning the surrounding jungle for signs of anyone approaching. Whether it was the AFP or his two friends, he wanted to be close to one of his captors when it all kicked off. Dindo unwittingly obliged, drawn to the group by the allure of Vick's beauty. He stood off to one side of her, glancing her way now and again, and both Grant and Vick knew that he was trying to get a glimpse down the front of her tattered T-shirt. Vick did nothing to obscure his view, lest he become embarrassed or angry. The last thing she needed was to lose her only real supply of nourishment, so she leaned forward a little, giving Dindo a better view of her cleavage while she chatted to Moore.

Grant judged the time to be about midday, which meant it would be another few hours before Sonny and Len were likely to turn up. With that thought still in his head, his heart sank as he saw a large *banca* appear at the mouth of the cove and throw out its anchor. Bong ordered everyone to prepare to move out and the guards starting packing everything away. The rice which was bubbling away in the pot was dumped unceremoniously onto the fire, extinguishing the flames while at the same time dealing yet another blow to the hostages' morale.

Grant frantically sought a way to avoid boarding the boat, but the only way he saw that happening was if he was dead, so he stood when ordered to and took his place in the line as they marched the last few hundred yards to the beach. A small motorised inflatable had been dropped over the side and was chugging towards the shore when they reached the sand and the first of the hostages were ordered to climb aboard, which they did awkwardly with their legs tied together. When the first four were in they were joined by two guards who ferried them to the *banca*, then they returned to escort the next lot across. Grant, Vick, Moore and Halton were the last hostages to climb into the dinghy and Sam wondered if it would be possible to overpower the crew once on board, but again his idea was dashed as he climbed onto the larger vessel and saw four more armed men watching over the group of hostages already aboard.

Resigned to the journey, he sat down next to Halton and prayed they had a well-stocked galley on board.

Chapter Eight

Wednesday 18 April 2012

Sonny gazed out of the tiny window at the sea far below and wondered what the fishing would be like in those waters. The island
of Jolo was just a few minutes away and yet another glance at his
watch told him that it was approaching seven in the evening. The
return journey from Farrar's office to the airport had been as tor-
turous as the initial drive over, and once they'd passed through
the diplomatic channel the news had been broken that the plane
was suffering a technical fault in the avionics. The resulting
delay meant they didn't arrive in Zamboanga City until five in the
afternoon, by which time Farrar had been in touch with the latest
developments.

'I got the call from Abu Sayyaf but they didn't use Sam's
phone, so we have no way of updating his current position.
However, he did manage to tell me he was on a boat heading
south-west, which means his most likely destination is Jolo.'
He'd pronounced it 'Ho-lo' just as the locals did. 'Once you touch
down in Zamboanga you can catch a connecting flight to Jolo.
Be warned, though, there is a US base close to the airstrip and
I don't think they'd take kindly to you turning up armed to the
teeth. Once you arrive, flash your new credentials, bribe them,
do whatever you have to, just get the hell out of there before the
military take an interest in you.'

With that advice ringing in his ears, Sonny had booked them two seats on an AirPhilExpress DHC-8 for the thirty-five-minute flight.

The plane touched down on the single airstrip and taxied to the gate, where any concerns they had about customs inspections proved unfounded. Once outside they flagged down a battered taxi and asked to be taken to the Bud Dajo trail.

Bud Dajo is a volcano rising out of the centre of the island to a height of just over two thousand feet. Its last eruption was over a hundred years ago, and while it was considered active there was little chance of it going off in the next few days.

It was dark by the time they reached the beginning of the trail, and as expected there were no other visitors to worry about. They paid off the taxi driver, who insisted he would be happy to wait for them, but Sonny declined the offer. He even offered his services as a guide up the mountain but Sonny insisted they knew the way and he reluctantly drove off into the night.

Once the headlights had disappeared they began changing, swapping their tourist clothes and comfortable shoes for field uniforms made from Disruptive Pattern Material, and sturdy hiking boots. The DPM had an IRR (Infrared-Reflective) coating, which made the wearer less likely to be spotted by anyone using night vision devices aimed at detecting infrared signatures. Donning their own night vision goggles and cradling their suppressed MP5SDs, they set off up the trail, maintaining a moderate pace to ensure they didn't alert anyone to their presence.

Having studied a Google map of the island, they'd agreed that the most likely landing place for Sam and the others would be the north end of the island, and from there they would most likely head inland, so the plan was to get to high ground and from there make a night sortie to try to locate their friend. Should that fail, they would wait until they got an update the following afternoon and close in on the latest location.

It was midnight by the time they got to within a hundred feet of the summit and found a good location for their lying-up point. After snacking on sandwiches they'd purchased at the airport they cleaned their weapons and set off back down the side of the conical volcano, this time heading north. With their M4 assault rifles slung over their shoulders they walked slowly, Sonny on point with his Heckler & Koch at the ready. Ten yards behind him Len scanned the area to their sides, occasionally turning to check their six. An hour into the search they came across a building and stopped twenty yards short to check it out. It was built on stilts, with the floor raised three feet off the ground. There appeared to be no sign of movement. After a ten-minute wait, Sonny edged closer while Len covered his advance. It took another few minutes to cover the ground, then Sonny popped his head round the corner and returned to signal the all clear. Len joined him and saw that they'd come across a storage hut, piled a couple of feet high with coconuts. With no sign of any targets they took a quick drinks break before Len took his turn on point.

For a further two hours they snaked their way through the jungle without coming across anything larger than a cockatoo and finally they agreed to head back to their temporary camp and get some shuteye.

Daylight was barely four hours away, and they took a more direct route back up the mountain, little realising that at one point they passed within two hundred yards of Sam as he once again tried to get some sleep with only a tree for a pillow.

It had taken just over six hours for the boat to cover the one hundred and fifty kilometres from Basilan to Jolo. When they arrived at the deserted beach just after dark they were again transferred ashore using the inflatable. If the *banca* had a galley on board Sam and the other hostages were not on the dining list, and once they began the march into the jungle he knew it would probably be the next day before they got another bite to eat. All the while he kept close to Dindo in anticipation of an AFP attack, hoping he could take out the young Muslim with his hidden shiv and grab his weapon to aid his escape. Unfortunately, no such attack took place, and at around eleven in the evening they arrived at yet another temporary camp, but one which was vastly different from the others he had been in.

The first difference was the number of terrorists he saw, close to two hundred by his estimate. There were also boxes galore and all of the weapons on view looked like they'd just come from the factory. As they entered the camp they passed a huge pot of rice and a selection of cooked meats, although he couldn't tell which animal they'd come from. Given his current hunger he wouldn't have cared if it had once been a horse's arse, and their spirits were raised when they were told to sit and bowls of rice and meat were handed round. It wasn't exactly a banquet but he could see from the smiles on the faces of the other hostages that it was the best they had eaten in a long time.

Grant was watching a group of men who were gathered around a box deep in discussion, torches masked with red tape illuminating a drawing of some kind. It looked to him like one of the many Chinese parliaments he had taken part in while on operations, when his small squad would evaluate a situation and all offer their opinions, regardless of rank. He popped another piece of horse arse into his mouth just as the group broke up and started to walk towards the huddled hostages, causing him to stop mid-mastication.

Two of the men were taller than the others, their attire different and their features Arabic. Grant's entire body froze as he stared at the face of the man he'd been researching for the last nine months, the man who had effectively ended the life of Tom Gray.

After he'd left his hospital bed in Subic Freeport, the first thing Grant had done was get Internet access. Farrar had agreed to it and had provided the laptop, but only after reminding him that his old life was over and he shouldn't try to contact anyone from the past. Having learned a lesson from the Tom Gray saga, where communication had been done with dead-drop emails—those that were written and saved as drafts but never sent, therefore never leaving an electronic signature—Farrar had set up security privileges on the machine so that it refused to load the websites of any email providers. Grant also suspected it contained a key-logging programme, which would record every stroke on the keyboard. Unfortunately, his knowledge of computers wasn't advanced enough to check for such software, and searching for help online would just alert Farrar to his intentions if any were installed. Instead, Grant had worked on the assumption that everything he did was being monitored.

The first search string he had entered into Google was 'Tom Gray', and wasn't surprised to see the search engine's announcement that there were 'about 3,500,000,000 results'. His first port of call was the BBC news website where he first discovered the name of the man suspected of attacking him. Abdul Mansour had also been suspected of killing a pensioner in a nearby village as part of his escape plan, although he had spared the lives of an ambulance crew he'd taken hostage. According to their testimony, it was so that they could let the world know who had been responsible for the attack. Grant then did a search for Abdul Mansour and judging by the number of search results returned, Grant guessed he'd gotten the message across. He found reports on Mansour's background, from growing up as Ahmed Al-Ali in Ladbroke Grove, London, to his reported activities in Afghanistan and Pakistan both before and after the attack in Sussex.

Grant immediately recognised Abdul Mansour and had to use all his willpower not to stare at him as he came to a stop and surveyed the hostages. His whole body was tense, not with fear but with the rising anger he felt at meeting the man who had tried to kill him. He'd anticipated this day would come, but not under these circumstances. He'd expected to be the hunter rather than the prey, or at least be armed with more than a pointy stick when they met.

Mansour stood over the group and played the light over them. His eye was drawn to Grant.

'We have no more need for these people,' Assaf said. 'Guarding them will be a waste of men, and we no longer need the money they will bring us.' He gave some orders and his men moved in.

'Not so hasty, my friend,' Mansour said, holding out his arm. 'They have more than just a monetary value. After we attack the base on Friday night, the Army will come at us in numbers, but they will be handicapped if we still have these hostages. They put a high value on human life and that is a weakness we will exploit.'

'Besides ...' He was staring at Grant, who saw the same look Vick Phillips had been giving him for the last couple of days.

'What's your name?' Mansour asked.

'Sam.'

Mansour searched his memory for the name but came up blank. 'You look familiar.'

'He gets that a lot,' Vick said, but her comment was ignored.

There was something about this man that had Mansour looking back over the last few years, yet nothing would come to mind. He gave up the mental search but took a moment to weigh the man up. By the look of him he must have been picked up quite recently, and many in that position were usually still in a state of shock at this stage, yet he had an air about him, something that said he wasn't too uncomfortable in these surroundings.

'What do you do for a living?' he asked Grant.

While his new looks might hide his past, Grant knew that his voice would be the one giveaway and he tried to keep his answer as short as possible.

'I make websites.'

There! That voice! He recognised it from somewhere, but just exactly where, he didn't know. He asked a few more questions but each time Grant answered in as few syllables as possible, and Mansour guessed there was a reason for this, but what? Had they met before?

The more he stared, the further away the truth seemed to be, so Mansour walked away. He was sure the answer would come to him, but if it didn't arrive soon he would have to do something about this 'Sam'.

Once he'd gone Vick inched closer to Grant.

'Tom,' she whispered.

Grant turned to face her and immediately realised what he'd done.

'I knew it! You're Tom Gray!'

Grant gestured for her to keep her voice down, knowing that denying it would be futile.

'Oh, my God! I thought you were dead!'

'That was the plan,' Grant said. 'How did you know?'

She took a moment to compose herself, still shocked at the discovery she'd made. 'I may be a travel writer but in order to pay for my trips I write for several publications. When you released your justice bill last year I was one of those opposed to it, and wrote an article explaining why it was a non-starter. I did a lot of research on you, including watching your appearances on the news over and over again. That's where I knew your voice from.'

'That's it?'

'No, the voice was only part of it. When you saved me from that bullet I knew you were no ordinary business owner, and I saw the look on Abdul Mansour's face when he walked up to you. I think he's close to recognising you, too. Maybe it's a good job the explosion altered your appearance somewhat.'

'You know who he is?' Grant asked.

'Are you kidding? After he attacked you his face was all over the news. He's more notorious than Osama Bin Laden.'

'Look, you have to forget about Tom Gray. I mean, you have to forget about me being Tom Gray. It's complicated, but if you tell anyone I'm alive, they'll kill the both of us. Now eat your food.'

'But who would want to kill you?' she persisted.

It was a conversation he didn't want to have, but she had to know the danger she had stumbled into, a danger greater than her current situation.

'Think about it. The government announced my death to the whole world. How happy do you think they'd be if you proved they had lied, eh? They know where I am right now, and if you ever mention my name and link me to this place they will know you are telling the truth. Oh, they'll dismiss you as a crackpot, saying it was post-traumatic stress disorder or something similar brought on by your ordeal, but they won't risk someone believing you and reigniting the fire.'

'They wouldn't do that,' she insisted. 'That only happens in books and films, not real life. The British government doesn't murder its own people.'

'Don't be so naïve. The government as a whole might not sanction it, but individuals will do all they can to hold on to their power. If anything threatens their position they will do all they can to eliminate the danger.'

'Then why did you agree to the name change?'

'I didn't agree, not at the time. I only found out about it when I woke from a coma two months after the attack, and by then the choice was either to accept the new life or go back to sleep permanently. They even performed plastic surgery to make me look even less like Tom Gray. I'm banished from the UK, I can't contact anyone from my past, and I didn't get a real say in any of it. If they can do that to someone who had such a high public profile, they wouldn't hesitate to silence someone who—and I mean no disrespect—they've never heard of.'

'But I don't understand. Why keep you alive if you are such a thorn in their side?'

'That was one of my first questions, and it seems some friends of mine had them over a barrel. I don't know the full details, but they negotiated a deal whereby I get a new life and the government's lies aren't exposed. I guess it would have been easy enough to get rid of me, but to silence my eight friends too would have been a red flag to the conspiracy theorists.'

'I see,' Vick said. 'That's gotta suck.'

'As I said, I didn't have a choice. And if we don't get out of here sharpish it's going to suck a whole lot more.'

'What's your plan?'

'Not a plan, as such. A couple of friends are on their way to get me and we just need to be ready when they get here.'

'Baines and Smart! I knew those names were familiar! They were part of your team last year, weren't they?'

'That's right, and hopefully they'll be here sometime tomorrow. When it all kicks off you need to do exactly as I say, you understand?'

Vick nodded and Grant reminded her to tell no-one, but she wasn't going to let it lie.

'I'm a writer, Tom, and this is absolute gold. I can't just pretend I don't know about the story of the century.'

'Just leave it,' Grant said, throwing her a look and signalling the end of the conversation. A few minutes later his guard arrived with the handcuffs and he settled down to another night of broken sleep.

Chapter Nine

Thursday 19 April 2012

While Grant's sleep was disturbed by the constant feeding of the indigenous insects, Abdul Mansour was kept awake by the gnawing sensation that comes from being one step away from total recall.

The fact that he couldn't put a name to the face had weighed heavily on him, and with it came a sense of foreboding. He wasn't a superstitious man, but he trusted his instincts, and right now they told him that there was something dangerous about this man.

These thoughts troubled him throughout his morning prayers and continued as he ate his breakfast, and once he'd finished he decided that the best thing to do would be to rid himself of the man, just to be on the safe side. However, having made that decision he found himself reluctant to go through with it.

Looking over at Grant, he knew he was so close to the truth, yet it was always a few inches from his grasp. If he killed the man and then subsequently made the connection it would be too late to do anything about it, yet his head said the man had to go.

After another hour of going round in circles he opted to settle the matter once and for all.

'Brother,' he said to Abu Assaf, 'the prisoner, Sam Grant, troubles me deeply. I feel it is not safe to keep him alive.'

'Troubles you? In what way?'

'I don't know,' Mansour had to admit, 'but it would be safer for all of us if he was no longer with us.'

Assaf shrugged and called over one of his men. 'Bong, take Grant into the jungle and dispose of him. Do it quietly.'

Bong Manalo nodded and went to find a couple of helpers, and together they approached the group of prisoners. Having already finished their breakfast, the hostages were lounging around in anticipation of the inevitable daily march through the jungle.

Bong stood over Grant and ordered his compatriots to remove the tether attaching him to Halton.

'Get up,' Bong said, 'you're coming with us.'

Grant did so, warily. 'Where are we going?' he asked.

'For a walk.'

Grant looked down at Halton, who averted his eyes and dropped his gaze to the ground. The simple gesture told Grant all he needed to know. This was one of those walks Vick had told him about, where four go out but just three come back.

He thought quickly and decided not to make a fuss here, not with a few dozen armed men to deal with. Instead he would go quietly and take his chance with his three escorts. Two of them carried their brand new M16 rifles while Bong was holding his *bolo* and had a pistol tucked into a hip holster. For his own part, Grant could feel the shiv up against his right calf and knew the time to use it was drawing close.

As they walked towards the edge of the clearing, Vick returned from her visit to the toilet in time to see Grant being led away. When she asked Halton what was going on she got the same response he'd given Grant and she immediately chased after the small group.

'No!'

She was quickly grabbed from behind and dragged back to the group of hostages, but she managed to scream one more time before a hand across the mouth silenced her and a *bolo* appeared at her throat.

'If you make another sound you will take a walk as well. Do you understand?'

With tears running down her face she nodded, never taking her eyes off Grant's back as he finally left the clearing and was led down a track and out of sight.

———⌣———

After grabbing a couple of hours sleep each—one napping while the other took watch—Sonny and Len set off back down the mountain in search of their friend. They retraced their route from the previous night for about a kilometre before peeling off to the right towards another hill. The sensible thing for Abu Sayyaf to do would be to seek the high ground and that was where Sonny and Len expected to find them, though as the landscape undulated relentlessly it was hit and miss as to which hill they should target.

An hour into their trek, Sonny wasn't sure if the sound he'd heard had been a woman's distant scream or just another of the animal sounds that continually assaulted the ears. The noise had come from his left and he looked back to see if Len had heard it, too. His friend indicated the direction the sound had come from and that told him that it wasn't his imagination.

Sonny took the lead and upped the pace slightly, balancing speed with the need to remain undetected. The origin of the sound he'd heard would be around a click-and-a-half away, he figured, which meant close to the top of the hill they were now approaching. Once within sight of the summit he slowed the pace and Len closed the formation, the pair inching closer while scanning the bush ahead for signs of movement.

Sonny's hand went up and Len froze, following the direction of Sonny's finger as he indicated two figures approaching fifty yards ahead. They both recognised their friend from the videos they'd been shown, and they guessed the man holding the long knife was his captor. Moments later two armed men came into view and the four continued their slow march towards the bottom of the hill. As the men passed, Sonny and Len gave them a thirty-second start before moving onto their tail.

They followed for another hundred yards before their targets stopped and Grant was shoved onto his knees. The two armed men moved aside to give the man with the knife some room, their rifles hanging loosely by their sides, muzzles pointing towards the ground.

Sonny indicated these two and showed which one he intended to take out, leaving the other to Len. They would then both concentrate on the man with the knife.

With his target in his sights, Sonny applied pressure to the trigger until the firing pin was released to send the round on its way.

Nothing.

A click, but nothing more. He quickly cleared what he assumed was a misfire and took aim again, but once more he got nothing more than a click as the firing pin hit the dud bullet.

Len had been waiting for him to take the first shot, taking that as the signal to take out his own target, and when he heard Sonny clearing his weapon for a second time he looked over to see what the problem was. All he got in response was a shrug and a finger to indicate one more attempt. Len nodded and took aim again but the shot he was waiting for never came.

Another glance over and he saw that Sonny had abandoned the silenced MP5 and was now readying his M4 Carbine. Sonny indicated that Len should try to take out the armed men and he would support him if things got loud.

Accepting the lead role, Len got a bead on the target farthest from him, exhaled and took the shot.

Click.

'What the fuck ...?'

One weapon misfiring was unusual, but two just never happened. They'd stripped the guns down the previous evening and all of the moving parts were in perfect working order, which left just the ammunition. He ejected the next cartridge in the breach and used his knife to pry the round from the casing, expecting black powder to pour out. Instead he ended up with a tiny pile of sand in the palm of his hand.

He could hear their friend's voice through the half-dozen trees separating them and knew time was running out. Inching sideways, he crept towards Sonny and told him what he'd found.

'Is all the ammo the same?' Baines whispered.

'Not sure.'

To answer his own question, Baines ejected a round from his own M4 and prised the bullet free, revealing yet more powdery sand.

'This was done deliberate,' Baines said. 'The question is, why?'

'No time for that now,' Len said, discarding all of his weapons except for his knife. 'We'll have to go hand-to-hand.'

Baines put a hand on his shoulder. 'What about playing rabbit?'

Len considered it for a moment, then nodded and made to get up. Baines grabbed his arm and pulled him back down.

'Rabbits are young and fit, not old, fat and bald,' he said to Len. 'Let me be the bunny; you catch them as they follow me.'

'Cheeky sod,' Len said, but had to concede that he'd put on a few pounds in the last year, and while he was not exactly bald, his hairline had been receding since just after puberty and there was nothing he could do about it. Sonny often joked that he looked more like a managing director than a soldier, but then occasionally he thought Sonny was a pillock, which evened things out.

Len crawled back from their vantage point to seek a decent hiding place, and after finding a tree trunk wide enough to hide his frame he indicated in which direction Baines should run and got into position.

Grant marched slowly down the hill with his two armed escorts behind him and Bong leading the way. After a couple of hundred yards Bong stopped and one of the guards put a hand on his shoulder and forced him onto his knees. Grant didn't offer any resistance as he'd anticipated the action and saw it as the chance to grab his shiv from his sock. With his hand on the shank he sat facing his executioner.

'You don't have to do this,' he said, glancing over at the two armed guards who had moved off to the right-hand side of the track. They were at ease, their guns pointing to the ground, but they could bring them up and have him in their sights within a second. 'The money is on its way. Why don't you just wait for it and let me go?'

Bong remained impassive. 'I have my instructions.'

No emotion, just the simple acknowledgement that taking this life would mean no more to him than taking out the garbage or mowing the lawn.

'Why don't you come with me, all three of you? You could share the money between you. You won't have to live in the jungle anymore and no-one will tell you what to do.' He added just the right amount of panic to his voice, letting them believe to the end that he was a man with no fight in him.

'I don't care about money. All I care about is a free Muslim nation, and Allah will provide that.'

'Then why kidnap me if you don't want the money?'

Bong sighed like a parent trying to explain the workings of the internal-combustion engine to a three-year-old. 'The money we made from you was supposed to help our cause, but now we have more than enough.'

Grant looked over at the other guards. 'What about you two? Wouldn't you like a million dollars between you?'

'They don't speak English,' Bong said. 'And even if they did, their loyalties lie with Allah. Now, have you anything else to say?'

'Yes. That man in your group, the foreigner, he's going to get you all killed. Believe me, I recognise him from the television and he was responsible for an atrocity in England last year. He recruited thirty local men and got them all killed while he got away.'

Bong let out a snort of derision. 'You think I fear death? No! It is coming to all of us and I will embrace mine so that I can finally fulfil my duty to Allah!'

He looked at his *bolo* and ran a finger along the sharp edge. 'You should embrace yours, too.'

As Bong took a step forward, Grant prepared himself. The *bolo* was hanging at Bong's side now, and he would have barely a second to get in close enough to use the shiv before his enemy had time to pull it back and counter the strike. Still, a second was a long time when the target was oblivious to the threat you posed. At least, that is what his training had taught him.

One more step . . .

A shout of pain pierced the jungle and all four of them looked towards the source of the noise in time to see a uniformed figure stumbling away from them. Grant recognised the gait and immediately knew that it was a diversion, one which his captors were falling for. The two guards immediately began firing as the retreating shape blended into the surrounding jungle, and a moment later they were off in chase. Bong raised his *bolo*, pointing at his two compatriots.

'Stop! Let him go!'

As he took a step towards them, Grant saw the chance and struck. He sprang up onto his feet and threw his left shoulder into

Bong's armpit, lifting him off his feet, while his right hand came round and plunged the point of the stick into the Filipino's neck. His momentum carried them for a couple of steps before he tripped on a tree root and they collapsed in a heap. Grant lay on the arm holding the *bolo* while he grabbed for the pistol in Bong's holster. He met no resistance; Bong was too busy dealing with the damage to his throat to bother about anything else.

With the pistol in his hand Grant swivelled towards the other two targets, flicking the safety off as he brought the weapon round in anticipation of them bearing down on him. He was surprised to see that they hadn't even noticed his attack, intent as they were on chasing their prey through the jungle.

He looked back down at Bong, who was clutching at the wound in his neck. He figured that the terrorist might survive if he got help quickly, and that wasn't something he wanted to happen.

'Live by the sword, die by the sword,' he whispered, and brought the *bolo* down hard, the sharp blade severing a few of Bong's fingers on its way to embedding itself in his spinal column. With one down and two to go, he set off in pursuit of the remaining threats. They were about twenty yards ahead, still pausing and firing every few steps, and he made up the ground quickly. He was within ten yards and had one of them in his sights when the leader passed a tree and an arm flashed out, catching him in the throat, sending both man and rifle clattering to the ground. The second terrorist stopped too, stunned at what he'd seen. He then saw a uniformed figure appear from behind the tree, stooping down to collect the weapon on the jungle floor. Raising his own rifle, he got the stranger in his sights and his finger began to squeeze the trigger.

Len saw the rifle being aimed at him and grabbed for the weapon at his feet, expecting to get the bad news any second. When the double-tap came he tensed for the impact, but none came. Instead, the remaining terrorist collapsed like a sack of bricks. As he went down Len saw Sam Grant standing a few yards beyond the body.

'I see the timing's still there,' he said, and gave his old friend a huge embrace. Sonny came jogging back through the jungle.

'Typical. I'm the one that gets shot at and Len gets all the hugs.'

He ignored the look he got from Smart and instead grasped Grant's hand and slapped him on the shoulder in a more macho welcome. 'Good to see you, Tom,' he said.

'It's Sam now.'

'Yeah, Farrar told us. It's going to be hard to get used to calling you Sam after all these years.'

'We can discuss that later. Right now we have to get moving. There's a couple of hundred heavily armed terrorists about half a click from here and all that shooting will bring them down on top of us.'

While Sonny and Len collected the weapons and ammunition from the fallen, Grant trotted back to Bong and went through the dead man's pockets looking for more ammunition. He found a spare clip, along with the mobile phone the Filipino had taken from him. When he rejoined the others, Sonny led them back in the direction of their LUP on the adjacent hill.

They moved quickly, desperate to put as much distance between themselves and anyone following. After a kilometre they stopped for a two-minute breather and checked their tail to see if anyone had latched on to it, but there was no sign of a pursuit.

'While I'm glad to see you guys, what the hell made you decide to turn up at a firefight without any weapons?'

'We had weapons, more than enough to do the job,' Len said. 'Trouble was, the ammo Farrar gave us was no good.'

'What do you mean by "no good"?'

Sonny removed the projectile from one of the 9 mm MP5 rounds and handed the cartridge over to Grant, who immediately recognised the problem. 'Are they all like this?'

'All the ones we've tried have been, and I can't see it being an accident.'

Grant let the sand trickle through his fingers. 'The question is, why? Why send you all the way here and then give you duff kit?'

'It looks like he didn't want the rescue to succeed,' Len offered.

'Possible, but then he could have just left you two at home and refused to pay a ransom. It doesn't make sense.'

'Maybe he was just sold some dodgy ammo,' Sonny said.

'Possible, but I doubt it.'

'Then let's go and ask him,' Len said to Grant. He was about to get up when he spotted the red dot moving up from Sam's shoulder to his temple.

'We've got company,' he said, and turned slowly to look in the direction of the laser sights.

'Let me see those hands. NOW!'

The good news was that the voice was American. The bad news, they realised, was that they had a whole lot of explaining to do.

The trio got to their feet, hands in the air.

'Walk towards me, slowly.'

They did as instructed and six figures emerged from the bushes, their camouflage having worked a treat. Five of them were Filipinos, while the sixth stood a foot taller.

'What the hell are you doing running around the jungle armed to the teeth?' the tall man asked as he approached, weapon still trained on them. When he got no answer he instructed his men to gather up the weapons and frisk their prisoners. The quick body searched produced two knives, a couple of 5.56 mm magazines and their mobile phones and comms gear.

After a quick conversation on his radio the leader of the group motioned with his gun. 'Okay, get moving.'

'Where are you taking us?' Grant asked.

'Our base is just a few clicks from here. My boss wants to ask you a few questions.'

———————

At the first sound of gunfire Assaf had sent his aide and a dozen men to investigate, and they returned twenty minutes later.

'They are dead, all three of them. The prisoner is gone.'

'The *sundalos*?' Assaf asked.

'I don't think so. Edgar was shot but Bong and Manny were killed with knives. The *sundalos* are cowards; they don't like to get in that close.'

Mansour was disturbed by what he was hearing. It seemed his instincts had been right all along, and he cursed himself for not disposing of the man with his own hand.

'Is it possible that the prisoner killed them?' he asked.

The aide considered the possibility. 'By himself? Unlikely. Two were stabbed and one was shot in the back of the head. I can't imagine how he could do that, especially when they managed to fire so many shots. He must have had help.'

Mansour frowned. If it wasn't the local soldiers, then who had come to his rescue? And what was so special about this man that someone would send in a team to retrieve him?

These concerns were soon pushed aside as he remembered having discussed the upcoming attack on the base in the man's presence. Should he bring this to Assaf's attention? He decided not to; Assaf would surely want to cancel the attack, and there was a schedule to maintain. Instead he took Nabil's arm and pulled him to one side.

'The attack will go ahead tomorrow, as planned, but there is a chance they may have been forewarned. You should expect heavy resistance.'

'If Allah wills it, they will all be sleeping in their beds. If not, I am ready to fight for my place amongst the virgins.'

'Allah will reserve a special place for you, I am sure of it.'

They rejoined Assaf. 'How are the preparations for the attack coming along?' Mansour asked.

'The vehicles have been purchased and we will be fitting them for the mini-guns this evening. Everything else is in place and the men know what is expected of them.'

'I would still like to get the team leaders together to go through the attack one more time.'

Assaf nodded and sent his aide to gather them together around the map table, which was nothing more than four crates pushed together to form a square.

'When the mounted unit goes in, you will have some extra company,' Mansour said. 'The Americans have a fondness for all things living, so we will place one of the white prisoners in each vehicle. We will need to ensure they are prominent, but not so much that they interfere with the mission. Any suggestions?'

He was hugely disappointed by the lack of response. How on earth were these people going to think on their feet in the middle of a battle if they couldn't come up with a solution to this simple problem? But then, the raid didn't have to succeed, it just had to be audacious and act as a warning to the western world.

'Nabil, what would you suggest?'

'The trucks we will be using have an open bed at the back. We could lash a board to the back of the cab so that it is pointing to the sky. We can then strap the prisoner to the board standing up, facing forward. They would be vulnerable to any incoming fire, which should cause our enemies to think twice before shooting.'

'I like it. Take some men and oversee the modifications to the trucks. Once they are completed we need to finish off the defences, so you will need to be quick.'

Nabil selected a couple of armed men to guide him down the mountain and another couple to help carry the mounting for the mini-guns and they set off through the morning heat. It was a three-hour trek to the compound where the trucks were being stored and he was soaked with sweat by the time he arrived, but he shrugged off the inconvenience and dived straight into the work.

The Dillon could be supplied with a DVRM-1 support assembly for mounting the weapon on the back of a vehicle, but aside from being bulky it was designed for use with the HMMWV, or Humvee class of vehicle. Instead they had brought along a couple of MK16 naval post mounts, designed primarily for naval deployment but capable of being mounted on any flat bed. All it required was an area of two feet by two feet—which the Datsun pickups had with room to spare—and Nabil began by marking out the bolt holes before drilling them out. He then used a rivet gun to secure the feet in place and moved on to the post for the prisoner. They settled on a couple of planks six feet long by eight inches wide and lashed them to the back of the cab vertically.

Once the modifications had been made they drove the trucks to a clearing a couple of kilometres from the base of the hill and climbed back to the camp. Mansour was standing with a group of others around one of the boxes and he was explaining how the Claymore mines worked when Nabil joined them.

'You are just in time,' Mansour said. 'I have been told that the perimeter foxholes have been completed. After you have eaten, I would like you to check them and start laying the defensive mines.'

'Certainly,' Nabil replied. A belly full of food was just what he needed, and afterwards he went to inspect the work that had been done.

The first foxhole he came across had half a dozen soldiers sitting around it and showed how much work remained to be done.

It was barely a scrape in the ground and the occupant couldn't have been more conspicuous if he'd painted himself fluorescent orange.

Nabil instructed one of the men to gather the others from around the perimeter and while he waited for them to return he gave the remaining soldiers instructions as to what he expected.

'This hole needs to be at least three feet from front to back and six feet wide. It also needs to be deep enough so that you can stand up in it with just your head and shoulders visible.'

He marked out the size with a stick and told them to start digging. While two took to that task Nabil showed the others how to create a roof for the hole using branches lashed together with thin strips of bark. The finished product looked like a coffee table, with an eight-inch leg in each corner. Nabil placed it over the finished hole and it had enough of a gap on the right-hand side that the occupants could get in without removing it. The final step was to camouflage it and he used cuttings from nearby bushes and ferns to disrupt the outline while allowing those inside a good field of fire.

Nabil pointed to one of the soldiers. 'Go and get another thirty men and tell them to bring shovels. The rest of you, follow me. I will mark out the locations for the other foxholes and I want four men working on each one. These have to be in place before we launch the attack tomorrow, so you will have to work fast.'

He paced out the distance to the next hole to ensure they weren't too far apart. If the enemy managed to overcome one of the positions he wanted the neighbours to be able to cover the gap. Once he'd done a complete circuit of the hill and returned to the original hole he had marked out ten positions and work had begun on each of them.

Next up was the laying of the Claymores. Unlike conventional mines, which are designed to be buried underground, these anti-personnel devices are command-detonated and directional, meaning they can target a certain area. The operator would wait until the enemy were in the kill zone before hitting the plastic detonator switch, sending around seven hundred 3 mm steel ball bearings out to a distance of a hundred yards, much like a giant shotgun. Anyone caught in the sixty-degree blast radius could kiss their shredded ass goodbye.

Nabil showed the men how to prepare the mine and disguise it, then ensured that the detonation wire leading back to the foxhole was buried under the dead leaves and other fallen debris on the jungle floor. Once back at the foxhole he demonstrated the trigger before attaching it to the wire, effectively priming the weapon.

Evening was drawing in as he finished the lesson. 'We need to make every hole the same as this one,' he said, 'and we don't have much time. After tomorrow's attack the enemy will come at us in great numbers, and these defences will be the only thing between survival and annihilation.'

Leaving them with that thought he returned to the camp for his evening prayers. As he neared the plateau he heard the familiar sound of gunfire coming from the opposite side of the hill. He flicked off the safety on his M16 and headed towards the noise.

Chapter Ten

Thursday 19 April 2012

Sister Evangelina Benesueda was concluding afternoon prayers, guiding the children through The Lord's Prayer for the second time that day. She had been running the tiny school virtually single-handedly for nearly a year since arriving from Manila and the work had been the most rewarding of her life.

It lifted her heart to see the happy faces of the orphans as they followed her lead, a few of them grappling with the English words but the majority comfortable with the new language.

> '... *Thy Kingdom come.*
> *Thy will be done on earth,*
> *As it is in heaven.*
> *Give us this day our daily bread.*
> *And forgive us our trespasses,*
> *As we forgive those who trespass against us ...*'

As they neared the end of the prayer Evangelina heard a commotion outside the front door and became wary. In a predominantly Muslim region, her Christian teachings attracted a lot of negative attention. This was the reason she had hired a local ex-policeman to stand guard outside during school hours, and it sounded like he was in a confrontation with someone.

She was walking towards the door just as it came crashing in and half a dozen armed men strode into the classroom. They were all brandishing *bolos* and two or three of them were already bloodied. Through the open door she could see her guard laid out on the floor, blood seeping from several wounds.

She saw the men eyeing the youngsters and ran to place herself between them, arms outstretched.

'They are just children!' she screamed, but her protests were cut off as a *bolo* arched through the air and connected with the side of her head, cleaving a gaping wound above her temple. A second blow caught her on the back of the neck as she fell and the last thing she saw was the kids being dragged, kicking and screaming, through the classroom door.

Camp Bautista is located next to Jolo's domestic airport runway and is home to the 3rd Marine Brigade, Philippine Marine Corps. Within the base is another compound which houses US troops, predominantly National Guardsmen. In addition, there is a detachment of the CIA's Special Activities Division.

In the battle against Abu Sayyaf, the US military had been given a strictly advisory role, assisting the local armed forces in terms of strategy and occasionally logistics. This directive hadn't sat too well with Colonel Travis Dane, commanding officer of the Special Operations Group which was the elite paramilitary element of SAD. As a man of action, sitting around in a comfortable office while just a few clicks away there were bad guys waiting to be killed was anathema to him. Being limited to arming and training the local soldiers had done nothing for his already formidable demeanour, leading the indigenous troops to give him the name Angry Dog. He was rather proud of his new tag and made sure everyone used it, even his own men. Perhaps because they shared his frustrations, he wasn't as hard on them as he was the rest of the world.

'Dog,' Scott Garcia said as he entered the office. 'The guys we found are in the cells.'

The Colonel got up from behind his desk and followed the sergeant over to the stockade.

'What do we know about them?'

'They're British, but they won't give me their names. One of them claims that Abdul Mansour is on the island preparing for an attack on the base.'

'Abdul Mansour? *The* Abdul Mansour, here on Jolo?'

Garcia shrugged. 'So he claims.'

As they entered the guardhouse the two Filipino guards snapped to attention.

'At ease.'

Dog saw the three men sitting in the single cell. A pile of personal belongings was on a table, including their phones. Dog powered them both up before thumbing through the contact lists in search of clues. One phone contained several Manila numbers and a few belonging to mobiles, while the other contained a single entry: Farrar.

'You want to tell me what you were doing in my jungle?' he asked the trio through the bars.

'We came to get our friend,' Len said, indicating towards Grant.

'So what's your friend's name?'

The question was met with silence.

'Okay, tell me about Abdul Mansour.'

'He's here on the island and is planning to attack one of the bases tomorrow night,' Grant said.

'This is the only base on Jolo,' Dog told him. 'We have a few people scattered across the island doing humanitarian work, but this is the main camp. So tell me how Mansour came to be on Jolo.'

'I don't know. I was captured by the Abu Sayyaf on Basilan last week and they brought me here yesterday. Mansour was already in their camp.'

'And he told you he was going to attack this base?'

'He didn't tell me personally. I overheard a conversation.'

'How can you be sure it was Abdul Mansour?'

'His face has been all over the news for the past year. I'd recognise him anywhere.'

Dog's expression conveyed his scepticism. 'Sorry, but I don't buy it. Mansour is a big-time player and if you told me he was going to attack the White House I might believe you, but to come to the poorest part of the world to attack a base housing less than a hundred US personnel is not his style.'

'Whether you believe me or not, it's going to happen,' Grant said, exasperated. 'You can either prepare for it, or ignore the warning and explain to your bosses why everyone under your command is dead.'

Dog let out a laugh. 'I hardly think a few dozen poorly armed terrorists are going to wipe out an entire base.'

'I'd say the number was closer to two hundred, and their weapons looked brand new. I think your intel needs updating.'

The size of the enemy force was clearly news to Dog, and it took a moment to process the new information. His team consisted of just half a dozen men, himself included, with the rest of the US contingent made up of eighty National Guard Engineers. There were also over a hundred Filipino marines assigned to the base. While they might be closely matched on numbers, he felt sure that training and experience would be the deciding factor. That was, if there was such a strong opposing force and they were actually planning an attack.

'We'll need to check this out,' he said. 'You said you were held in their camp; where is it?'

'Not far from where he found us,' Grant said, nodding towards Garcia. 'Head south for about one click, then start climbing. They're on a plateau about a hundred yards from the summit.'

He took his sergeant aside. 'Scott, does that sound plausible?'

Garcia pulled his operations map from his pants pocket and found the location. 'He could be telling the truth. Those directions put them on Hill 178, and we've had a few skirmishes in that area, though we've never managed to get close to the top. Drones haven't managed to tell us much, either.'

'Take your team and see how close you can get. Avoid contact if you can; just give me numbers.' Dog lowered his voice to a whisper. 'Before you leave, stop by the command centre and get close-up shots of these guys using the CCTV, then have them sent to Langley.'

Garcia nodded and left the room.

Dog sat on a desk and folded his arms. 'So, assuming you're telling the truth, I still need to know who you are. We're usually the first to be notified about kidnappings and there's been no reports of a white male being taken, not for a few months anyway. Why would that be?'

'Maybe because I didn't contact the embassy,' Grant shrugged.

'But you have had contact with the outside world,' Dog said, and turned his attention back to the phones. The operating system was unfamiliar so it took him a moment to find the call log.

As he was fiddling his way through the menus the door banged open and a five-foot storm barrelled into the room.

General Tomas B. Callinag, commanding officer of the 3rd Marine Brigade, had a reputation that made Dog look like an excited puppy. While Dog begrudged his unit's non-combatant role, Callinag resented their very presence on Philippine soil.

'When were you going to tell me about these prisoners?'

Dog stood lazily to attention, knowing his insubordinate actions would further rile the officer but caring little.

'I was just about to send a runner to inform you, sir.'

Callinag dismissed the excuse with a wave of his hand and stood in front of the cells staring at the occupants.

'Who are they? What are they doing on Jolo?'

'I was just in the process of establishing that, General. Would you mind if I continued?'

The Filipino shot him a look before moving away from the cell and settling into a chair behind the desk.

'You say you were kidnapped last week,' Dog continued, 'which means you could only have been communicating with someone called Farrar. And why did they let you keep your mobile, I wonder? It looks to me like you guys are members of Abu Sayyaf.'

'They didn't let me keep it,' Grant said indignantly. 'I took it back when I escaped.'

'Okay then, tell me about Farrar.'

'He's just someone I met in Manila. One of my captors saw his name in the phone and called him, that's all.'

'So how come your friends have a phone with just one contact in it: Farrar?'

Grant knew he had already said far too much, and just stared at the wall, indicating an end to the conversation.

Garcia popped his head round the door and nodded to Dog before disappearing as quickly as he'd appeared.

'Gentlemen, you might as well tell me who you are now. Your mug shots are currently being analysed at CIA headquarters in Langley and they will be able to cross-reference your details with every friendly intelligence agency in the world. Why don't you just—'

He was interrupted by the chirping of Grant's phone, and the display told him who was on the other end of the call.

'Let's see what Farrar has got to say about all this, shall we?'

'Put it on speakerphone,' Callinag said, 'I want to hear this, too.'

When the notification appeared on his laptop screen, Farrar clicked the message and saw that Grant's phone had been activated. Strangely, the device he'd given to Smart and Baines appeared to be in exactly the same location. Did it mean they had successfully rescued him already, or had they been captured by Abu Sayyaf, too?

He decided that the only way to find out was to call Grant's phone and see who answered.

'Hello?' he heard when the call was connected. Farrar didn't recognise the voice but it was definitely Filipino.

'Where is Bong?' he asked.

'Bong isn't here,' the voice said. 'Who is this?'

'It's Farrar. Is Sam still with you?'

'Yes, Sam is here, and so are two of his friends.'

Excellent, Farrar thought, giving himself a mental high-five. Knowing he had to temper his excitement for a little longer he took a couple of deep breaths.

'I think you should know that Sam and his friends are mercenaries working for the British government. They were sent to kill your leaders.'

'Farrar, you bastard—'

Smart's words told Farrar that his last statement had sealed their fate and a genuine smile appeared on his lips for the first time in weeks.

'Goodbye, Sam. I can't say it's been a pleasure knowing you.'

Farrar hung up the mobile phone and removed the SIM card, placing it in his pocket. He called his driver and told him to have the car ready in ten minutes, then asked his secretary to book him onto the next flight for London Heathrow.

With Grant and the others out of the way he had a few hours to shut down the Manila operation before heading home to Oxfordshire. The staff would be transferred to other duties and the offices would be handed back to the leasing company, all details which the attaché at the British Embassy would handle on his behalf. His sole concern was to get home to his apartment and pack his bags.

Picking up just his laptop and jacket, he walked out of the office for the last time, without giving his secretary so much as a 'goodbye'.

On the drive to his apartment he tossed the SIM card into the street where a thousand tyres would crush it to dust within the hour. When he arrived he told the driver to wait while he went inside to collect the few personal items he'd brought with him from the UK, mainly clothes and books.

With his suitcase packed it was time to head to the air-port, where his ticket was waiting at the Emirates Airline desk, and in the First Class lounge he relaxed with a twelve-year-old malt.

As he sipped the whisky he was thankful that the end of the operation was in sight. Just another couple of weeks and his career progression would advance another step closer to the top.

When the phone call ended Callinag demanded to know why the British government were sending kill squads to his island. The reply was rather succinct: 'That's bullshit!'

'We'll find out soon enough,' Dog said, stepping in to calm the situation. 'Once your files come back we'll know what to do with you.'

'I want to talk to you,' Callinag said, and Dog followed him out of the guardhouse.

'The bastard set us up,' Smart whispered once they'd gone, his anger apparent.

'Why, though?' Baines wondered.

'Pretty obvious, really,' Grant said. 'Very few people outside the government know that I'm still alive, and every single day brings the threat that one of us might break the news. It's something I've thought about for the last year, and I know what I would do if I was in their shoes: Get rid of us, permanently.'

'We considered that, too,' Smart admitted, 'but they can't kill us all. We agreed that if one of us dies in suspicious circumstances, the others would go to the papers with our story.'

'What if the deaths were above suspicion? Farrar told me that Tris died while on a mission in Iraq, and that happens in our line of work, so it didn't raise any alarm bells with me at the time. That means, of the seven of us that survived the attack last year, there are only six of us left. If Farrar had succeeded in getting us captured and killed by Abu Sayyaf there'd be just three.'

'Two,' Baines corrected him. 'Paul came off his bike a couple of months ago.'

'Fell off, or knocked off?' Grant asked.

'The back tyre blew while he was bombing up the motorway. Witnesses said there was no-one near him at the time. Trust me, we checked.'

'So with us out of the way there's just Jeff and Carl left, and the secret will die with them.'

'That's if they accepted that our deaths were not suspicious,' Baines pointed out.

'Of course they wouldn't be suspicious. They can hardly blame the British government if we were killed by terrorists in the Philippines, can they?'

The considered their position for a while, but no matter which way they looked at it they kept coming back to the same conclusion.

'Farrar's trying to bury the evidence—namely us,' Smart said.

The others agreed, and the discussion turned to their options. Baines wanted to turn the tables on Farrar but Grant was quick to point out that it was a waste of time.

'Farrar must have been taking orders from someone in power, someone near the top of the political ladder. If we take him out they will just replace him with someone else to finish the job.'

'So we take the fight to them?' Smart asked.

'It's that or spend the rest of our lives on the run.'

Baines began suggesting a plan of attack, the first stage of which was to grab Farrar and find out who was pulling his strings, but Grant was quick to dampen his enthusiasm.

'One step at a time. First we need to get out of here.'

The thought brought them all back to reality. With their photos winging their way to Langley it was only a matter of time before Baines and Smart were identified.

Grant was another story.

If the CIA cross-referenced with the British security services it was possible that a match might come back, but more likely the UK government wouldn't want to share the fact that Tom Gray was still alive.

They were considering their next move when Dog and Callinag returned.

'So, Mr. Baines, Mr. Smart, we now know a lot more about you than we did thirty minutes ago,' Dog said. He focused on Grant. 'You, however, remain a mystery.'

Grant simply looked away, not wanting to engage the man, and Dog was content to deal with the other two for the moment.

'Quite a past you guys have,' he said, reading from a print-out. 'Served in the SAS; saw action in Iraq; freelancers for the last five years; and co-conspirators with Tom Gray in the spring of last year.'

He looked up from the page. 'If you'd tried that stunt in the States you'd be on death row right about now. How come your government let you walk?'

'I guess the PM is a sucker for a pretty face,' Baines quipped.

Dog ignored the comment and turned his attention back to Grant. 'What about you? You're obviously British, and friends with these guys, yet your picture isn't listed on any database and the name Sam doesn't bring back any matches. How do you explain that?'

Grant maintained his silence, much to Callinag's annoyance.

'Answer the question!' he shouted, but Grant didn't so much as flinch.

'Don't worry, General, Langley is passing their details over to the Brits, so we should have a match real soon. In any case, they'll no doubt be sending someone to take them off our hands.' He flipped a lazy salute to the superior officer and took his leave.

It was four hours later when the reply from Langley came through. Dog looked at the printout and wondered just who the hell this man was, given that the page simply contained the name Sam Grant and the words TOP SECRET in big, bold letters. No matches in the CIA database—or any other database for that matter. NSA had turned up blank, as had the FBI, leaving just the concise response from the Brits.

Orders from Langley were to await their collection by a British team, ETA thirty-one hours.

Back in his office, and with his interest aroused, he spent the next two hours researching Baines, Smart and the whole Tom Gray affair, but there was no mention of a Sam Grant.

There was, however, a strong likeness between Grant and the image of Gray on his screen. Could this be the man sitting in his cell? It would explain the secrecy, especially as Gray was certified dead.

Internet searches for Sam Grant returned nothing that related to his prisoner, adding further weight to his burgeoning theory.

He printed off a photo of Tom Gray and was heading over to the guardhouse when one of his troopers caught up with him and flashed a salute.

'Sergeant Garcia has just reported in, Dog! He's taking heavy fire on Hill 178!'

'Casualties?'

'One dead. He's pulling his team back.'

Dog grimaced. Callinag wouldn't be happy that one of his men was down.

'Okay, tell Harrison to take two squads in support.'

The trooper nodded and ran off to relay the order, while Dog abandoned his trip to the cells and instead headed towards the command centre.

'What's the latest?' he asked as he entered.

'Garcia's pulling out. Confirmed one dead, one injured: a bullet to the leg. It's slowing their withdrawal.'

Dog grabbed a headset. 'Bravo One, Charlie Two, what's your situation, over?'

'We're half a click from the base of Hill 178, no pursuit at this time, over.'

'What's the enemy strength, over?'

'Upwards of thirty, small arms and mortars, over.'

It didn't sound like a typical skirmish. The numbers suggested a much larger concentration of enemy than they normally encountered.

Dog gave Garcia coordinates to an exfiltration point and ordered a medevac team to meet them there. With the team now out of danger he crossed the square to the guardhouse, formulating a plan as he walked.

Dusk was approaching, heralding a shift-change for the ubiquitous flying insects. He was thankful for the Army-issue repellent that would keep them at least eight inches from his skin, for a while at least.

Inside the stockade he took his usual seat on the corner of the desk and pulled out the printout he'd made, which had Tom Gray's photo and some notes he'd garnered from the Internet. Now and again he would look up at Grant, then back to the page.

'So, it looks like you did some time in the SAS, too, Sam Grant.'

He glanced over to the cell but the prisoner remained impassive. *Time to crank it up*, he thought.

'It also says you're single. Well, you are now that your alcoholic wife rammed herself into a bridge!'

Grant's jaw hardened at the remark, but it was Baines who gave the game away by leaping from his seat and grabbing the bars.

'She wasn't an alcoholic, you worthless shit!'

Dog dismissed the two Filipino soldiers on guard duty and once they were gone he strode over to the cell. 'Calm down, son, I didn't mean anything by it. I was just fishing, and I think I just caught me a Tom Gray.'

He looked at Grant, who offered no denial. Baines also turned to Grant and shot him an apologetic look.

'So what happens now?' Grant asked.

'Well, a team is en route to pick you up and take you back to England. In the meantime, why don't you explain what you're doing here, and what that phone call from Farrar was all about?'

'Wait! Who exactly is coming to pick us up?'

Dog shrugged. 'All I know is a team from the UK are on their way and they'll be here the day after tomorrow.'

The three men looked at each other. After a few moments it was Grant who made the decision and he told Dog the entire story, starting with Abdul Mansour's attack the previous year. He explained how all three came to be on Jolo and ended on Farrar's phone call and the implications it held for all three of them.

'I know you don't agree with what we did last year, but if you hand us over to them you'll be signing our death warrants.'

'That's where you're wrong. What you guys did took balls, but I couldn't say that in front of the General.'

'Then let us go.'

Dog shook his head. 'No can do. The best I can offer is to pass your concerns back to Langley and let them decide.'

Grant sprang to his feet. 'Are you fucking listening to me? If you mention the name Tom Gray to anyone, you'll be next on their list!'

Dog considered the statement, and with the story he'd just heard he knew it made sense.

'Okay, so I don't tell Langley. But that doesn't leave me with many options.'

'Well, we're fresh out of options, too,' Grant said. 'So I'll make this simple: if you hand us over to them, I'll tell them you know my real identity.'

He let the threat hang for a moment.

'Now find a way to get us out of here!'

Chapter Eleven

Thursday 19 April 2012

When the Emirates flight touched down in Dubai, Farrar was one of the first to disembark from the first class section. After the short walk to his connecting flight he turned his phone on and checked for messages. He was a nervous flyer and had happily complied with the stewardess once she informed him that it could interfere with the flight instruments.

There were seven voicemails, all from his boss, which suggested they weren't welcome home messages. His call was answered on the second ring, the voice exploding in his ear.

'Where the hell have you been?'

'I was on a flight, sir. What's the emergency?'

'What's the emergency? Well, let's see. The last communication I had from you said our three problems had been eliminated. So why did I receive a request for information about them from our American cousins? How do you explain the fact that they are being held at a US base on a remote southern Philippine island?'

Farrar's head was spinning. How could they still be alive? Did they escape, or did Abu Sayyaf let them go? As he pondered the likelihood of both scenarios, a third popped into his head: they hadn't been with Abu Sayyaf when he'd called.

'Are you still there, Farrar?'

His boss's voice brought him back to the moment. 'Yes sir, still here. I'll catch a flight back and sort this out personally.'

'Don't bother. I've sent a team to do the job. I couldn't wait around all day waiting for you to return my calls. You just get back here and report to my office as soon as you land.'

'Yes sir, I'll be there in ...,' but the line was already dead, and a sinking feeling in the pit of his stomach told him his future was heading in the same direction.

Damn you, Tom Gray!

He sat in the lounge fuming for what seemed an eternity, until self-preservation took over. Perhaps all was not lost. There was still a chance to redeem himself by personally making sure the remaining two hits were executed as planned. His failure in the Philippines could be explained away and once this mission was over he would make damn sure the next went without a hitch.

Once he boarded the plane he declined the offer of champagne, preferring instead to keep a clear head while he fabricated an explanation for his superiors.

'What makes you think Grant is telling the truth?' Dog asked Garcia towards the end of the debriefing.

He'd given his sergeant a rundown of the information received from Langley, but had stopped short of revealing Grant's true identity.

'These people were dug in, and dug in well.' Most of the encounters with the terrorists had taken place as they moved from one temporary base to the next, but this latest battle suggested a more permanent encampment.

'It still doesn't mean an attack is imminent, or that Abdul Mansour is on the island.'

Garcia had to agree, but said the shift in the enemy's Standard Operating Procedure suggested they were hunkering down.

'Maybe they just got sick of running,' Dog offered. 'Either way, it plays into our hands. We don't have to chase them all over the island and we can keep them contained on that hill indefinitely. If necessary we can starve them out.'

'They're bound to have hostages,' Garcia pointed out. 'We'd be starving them, too.'

'I've taken that into account. We offer food in exchange for the hostages and eventually they run out of bargaining chips.'

He could tell by the look in Garcia's eyes that something was bothering him and asked him to speak his mind.

'Well, they might refuse an exchange and instead start killing hostages until food is delivered. Their regard for human life isn't all that great.'

It was something Dog had considered, too, and to be fair to Garcia it was probably the most likely outcome. Grant's recollection of his time with Abu Sayyaf suggested they had just three western hostages and a handful of Filipinos. The locals would probably be the first to go, the American and two Brits being too valuable to simply kill. Having said that, they were quite willing to murder Grant and probably would have, had he not had any help. His planned execution came at a time when they thought a million dollars was on its way, which suggested their need for money wasn't as great as previously thought.

So what made them toss away a million bucks?

The question brought him back to Grant's sighting of Abdul Mansour, and he knew in an instant that the man was telling the truth. He shared his thoughts with Garcia, who concurred.

'He could be telling the truth about an attack, too,' Garcia said.

Dog nodded. If Grant was right, a couple of hundred terrorists were about to come charging out of the jungle. He'd need more than a handful of battle-hardened soldiers, some National Guard bridge builders and a heap of—in his opinion—poorly disciplined Filipinos if he was going to repel them successfully.

'Do we wait for them to launch an attack, or try to stop them before they get here?' Garcia asked.

'We don't have the men to go out and face them. In fact, we are going to be hard pushed to mount a solid defence within our own perimeter. I'll call SOCPAC and see what resources they have available.'

He rose from his chair and gestured for Garcia to follow him.

'Before I call this in I want to see if Grant knows what we will be facing,' Dog said as they crossed the square to the stockade.

The prisoners were just finishing up a meal when they entered, and Dog waited for the Filipino guards to clear away their dishes before dismissing them.

'Sam, you said an attack was about to take place on this base, and we believe you,' Dog said. 'We need to know what we're up against.'

'How many men, what weapons they have available, anything you can tell us,' Garcia added.

Grant told them what little he knew about the enemy's strengths. He had seen them brandishing new M16s and there were several ammo boxes dotted around the camp. There were also the multiple-shot RPGs, but he had no idea how many rounds they had for them. That was all he could be certain of. One or two of the boxes looked like they might contain more RPGs but he hadn't seen the contents, so he couldn't be sure.

'What else?' Garcia pressed.

'There were a few other containers but they were nondescript and could have contained anything from food to a small generator. Apart from the weapons, there's a couple of hundred bad guys and Abdul Mansour.

'How does that stack up against your defensive capabilities?'

'We're slightly outnumbered, but we know how to build a perimeter,' Garcia said confidently.

Baines wasn't impressed. 'I've seen Abdul Mansour in action, and he knows how to plan a coordinated attack at very short notice. Last year he took thirty kids off the streets, gave them AK-47s and managed to get through Tom Gray's defences, which included well-trained armed police officers. Imagine what he could do with two hundred armed men who've already seen their share of battle.

'So tell me, how many skilled troops do you have?'

'Six with combat experience,' Dog replied, 'plus another seventy National Guard and a hundred locals, give or take. They can all handle a weapon.'

'That may not be enough. Can you draw on anyone else in the region?' Smart asked.

'I'm heading over to speak to Special Operations Command Pacific. We'll have all the men we need by the time tomorrow night comes.'

He got up to leave, but Grant had some final words of warning.

'Don't underestimate him. Get them to send the best they have, and lots of them.'

When Nabil climbed back to the camp he found Mansour and Abu Assaf were waiting for him. The gunfire had lasted barely three minutes, and the battle was over by the time he'd got there.

'A small patrol,' he reported when they asked what had happened. 'I estimate five or six men. We killed one that we know of, and took no casualties of our own.'

Assaf shrugged off the incident. 'We have these skirmishes all the time,' he told Mansour. 'It is nothing new.'

'Perhaps,' Mansour mused, but something told him all was not well. 'How often do patrols come into this area?'

Assaf had to think about the question for a moment. 'The last time they ventured this close was about three months ago,' he admitted. 'Most of our encounters are in the lower regions, in the valleys and flatlands towards the edge of the forest.'

As the last of the twilight gave way to darkness, Mansour made his decision. 'The prisoner who escaped must have alerted the enemy, which is why they sent a scout party. We must bring forward the attack before they can prepare their defences.'

'You want to attack them in daylight?' Assaf asked, his expression suggesting he wasn't entirely happy with the idea.

'No, we must hit them tonight.' He turned to Shah. 'Nabil, have you prepared the defences?'

'Everything is in place.'

'Good, good.' To Assaf he said, 'Nabil will lead the attack. Gather your senior men and we will assign them their targets.'

Assaf called one of his men over and told him to assemble the others.

'I must leave tonight,' Mansour said. 'Please ensure the transport is ready to go in three hours.'

Assaf handed a phone to another soldier and told him to contact the boat owner with the updated schedule. As he did so, a group of men arrived at the camp with nine children in tow.

Nabil looked at Mansour questioningly. 'What are they doing here?' he asked.

'Just a little insurance, my friend. There is no telling how they will retaliate, and a few adult hostages might not be enough to stay their hand. They will think twice if they know there are children in harm's way.'

Nabil wasn't happy with the idea, but was not about to question Mansour's decision. Instead he offered to lead the briefing and with Mansour's blessing he went off to prepare the map of the base.

'The boat is on its way,' Assaf told Mansour. 'I will have my men escort you to the rendezvous point.'

Mansour thanked him for his hospitality. 'May Allah watch over you; I pray he doesn't need too many martyrs tonight.'

'Thank you, my brother. Will we see you again?'

'No. I cannot make this journey again, but I will send others in my place. You can be assured of our continuing support.'

He saw that Nabil was about to begin the briefing so he said a quick farewell.

'Once the attack is over I want you to make your way to Sumalata as planned.'

Sumalata, set in a bay in one of the seventeen thousand Indonesian islands, was a three-hundred mile journey due south.

'The vessel that brought us here should be able to make the journey in less than a day. I will have someone waiting onshore at one o'clock in the morning for the next seven days. If you don't arrive by then I will assume Allah's need was greater than mine.'

After a brief hug, Mansour—carrying his bag and an M16— joined the four armed men ready to guide him through the pitch black jungle. The *sundalos* never ventured into the jungle at night, one of them explained, but that did not prevent them from taking their time. One man took point a hundred yards ahead, ready to raise the alarm if necessary, but the trek passed off without incident.

As Abdul Mansour climbed aboard the *banca* he saw the sky on the horizon light up as mortars hit their targets, followed moments later by the signature *CRUMP!* and the chatter of distant small arms fire. Saying a prayer for his friend, he gave the order to cast off and began the next leg of his mission.

Chapter Twelve

Friday 20 April 2012

While Len and Sonny slept soundly on their bunks, Sam Grant lay awake staring at the ceiling. Despite the events of the past few days, it wasn't Farrar or Abdul Mansour that occupied his thoughts, but rather Vick Phillips.

In the short time spent in her company he had seen an inner strength that he'd found alluring, even more so than her considerable physical attributes. She had obviously been deeply affected by the death of the Filipino girl and her parents shortly after her capture, and the constant run-ins with the local forces must have taken their toll, too. Still, she remained resolute, determined not to let the situation completely overwhelm her.

If only Dina had managed to find such courage following Daniel's death, they might still be together, but she simply hadn't been prepared to deal with the tragedy. Her life had been an easy one, brought up with private schooling and all the privileges her parents could bestow, whereas he had been dragged up on a South London council estate and had fought to survive from a very early age. They were as different as could be, and it came as no surprise when Dina's parents objected to the engagement. The fact that he was coming to the end of his military career went some way to appeasing them, and when his business took off his star rose a little higher, but there was always the underlying class gap that he couldn't seem to overcome.

He had loved Dina, of that there was no doubt, but they were from different worlds. She had never been more than dutiful in the bedroom. It was as if love-making was just a necessary—and not entirely pleasant—part of the pregnancy process. Following the birth of their son Daniel the passion had almost completely disappeared, with her focus turning to the needs of their child.

The short relationship with Alma had been much the same to this point. The physical aspect aside, his own passion had been on the wane as with every passing day he realised just how little they had in common.

With Vick, though, it was different. They had spent only a couple of days together, but during their snatched conversations in their rest periods he had felt a real connection. They were both physically active, enjoying running and cycling, and they had similar tastes in music, books and films. An only child, she had never married and had infrequent contact with her parents, who had retired to Australia a few years earlier. She had been offered the chance to go with them but had turned it down in order to continue her career in journalism.

He tried to push thoughts of Vick out of his mind. He was with Alma now, but as he considered their relationship the realisation hit him: he could never return to his Manila home. His life in the Philippines was over, and Alma was not the kind of person who would be suited to a life on the lam. He would do what he could to ensure that she was taken care of financially, but he knew he could never see her again.

His thoughts once again turned to Vick, and he knew it would not be fair to drag her any further into his business. Despite his feelings for the girl, he knew he had to steer clear of her lest she become embroiled in the fight which lay ahead.

His priority was to get out of the cell. After that he had to get word to Jeff and Carl to let them know they were in danger. Beyond that, he didn't know, but he wasn't willing to spend the rest of his life looking over his shoulder.

He was in the process of figuring out the next step when the first mortar round hit the fuel dump a hundred yards from the guardhouse. The shockwave almost picked the building up, and all three were thrown from their bunks. Len and Sonny instinctively scrambled for their weapons, but they soon remembered where they were and realised they had nothing to protect themselves with.

The solitary guard rushed to what was left of the window and looked out at the devastation just as another shell fell in dead ground.

'You have to let us out of here!' Grant shouted. 'Those rounds are getting closer!'

The guard ignored him and stuck his rifle through the broken window frame, desperately searching for a target. The sound of small arms fire could be heard between mortar blasts, and the tree line beyond the runway sparkled with each incoming bullet.

'Hey! You have to let us out!'

Len and Sonny joined in, all three trying to get the guard's attention, but his focus was on the attackers. He let off a five-second burst towards the trees but all he managed to do was empty his magazine. As he fumbled for another he suddenly became aware of the prisoners shouting at him.

'Let us out!'

He grabbed the keys from his belt but rather than open the cell he simply looked from the men to the keys, back and forth, wondering if it was such a good idea. Before he could make a decision another mortar round burst a few yards away, showering the hut with red-hot shrapnel. The guard, standing too close to the already shattered window, took the brunt of the force. His shredded body hit the opposite wall and bounced to the floor a few feet from the cell.

Grant tried to grab the keys but they were tantalisingly out of reach. He looked around for something he could use to extend his reach but nothing seemed available, so he whipped off his T-shirt and tried to snag it on the keys in the dead guard's hand. Again and again he tried, but with no luck.

The next shell to land in the camp gave him the help he needed, destroying the guardhouse door and sending chunks of wood in his direction. Grant grabbed a piece around three feet long and finally managed to wrest the keys from the corpse.

He opened the cell and they poured out, looking for weapons. The guard had his M16 but there was nothing else in the room.

'We need to find the Colonel,' Len said, snatching the weapon up and inserting a fresh magazine taken from the Filipino's pocket.

The others followed him to the door and they took in the situation. A truck was on fire away to their left, caught in the blast that had devastated the fuel dump. Three other buildings were also alight and others had suffered bomb damage. Several Filipino soldiers were firing blindly into the tree line from behind whatever cover they could find, while a few lay dead, having been caught out in the open during the initial barrage.

Sergeant Garcia was trying to get a defence organised and the American troops were doing their part, but his efforts were hampered by the inexperienced local troops, who ignored his orders and continued to fire ineffectively at targets they couldn't see.

Grant pointed to a building with several antennae on the roof. 'Comms building,' he said, and they all moved towards it at speed. They had to break cover twice but made it safely to the building just as Dog emerged with his rifle. The surprise on his face was obvious but there wasn't time for explanations.

'We need air support,' Grant said as he led the group behind the shelter of the building. 'The fire is coming from the trees. What have you got in the air?'

'Nothing local. I called it in but SOCPAC say it will be at least forty minutes before they can get anything overhead.'

'We'll be lucky to last ten minutes,' Len said, a feeling shared by the others.

'What about heavy weapons?' Grant asked.

'We have mortars but they don't have the range to be effective.'

'So how come theirs can reach us?' Sonny asked.

Dog led him to the side of the building and pointed towards the chain link fence separating the base from the runway. 'On the other side of the airstrip there's Junk Town, built from scraps of corrugated iron and anything else the locals can lay their hands on. They must be holed up in there.'

'We need to clear them out. Can you spare a couple of men?'

Dog got on the radio and two of his troops were with them within thirty seconds. The pair couldn't have been more different. One looked like he'd come straight from a Mr Universe contest, while the other had a similar frame to Sonny—only without the good looks.

'Harrison, Keane, I need you to clear Junk Town. You're looking for mortar teams, number unknown.'

'I'll go with them,' Baines said.

'I can't sanction that. You stay here.'

'Sonny was a CRW instructor for three years,' Grant said. 'No-one does house-to-house better.'

Dog thought for a moment, then nodded. He had been through the Counter-Revolutionary Warfare programme whilst on secondment to Hereford a few years back, and knew how good you had to be to pass the course, never mind teach it.

To Keane he said, 'Grab their weapons from the command room and bring three comms units.'

The soldier disappeared and was back within a minute, doling out the equipment as well as ammunition. Len handed Grant the M16 as well as a spare magazine, preferring the Heckler & Koch. With everyone geared up, Keane led Harrison and Baines to the main gate to make their circuitous approach to the shanty town. Meanwhile, Dog surveyed the chaos inside the camp.

'We need to help the Sarge get the defence organised,' he said, nodding towards Garcia.

They ran from cover and Dog sprinted over to Garcia, who was still struggling to get the Filipino marines to conserve their ammunition and pick their targets. A few National Guardsmen were scattered around the camp, but not as many as Grant had expected to see.

Smart peeled off to the right while Grant took the left and dropped himself between two Filipino soldiers. The shock on their faces barely had time to register before he broke into tutor mode. He tried explaining that they should conserve ammunition but got blank stares in return, so he mimed the actions as he spoke.

'Ba-ba-ba-ba-bang! No good!' he said, making the universal 'cut-it-out' motion with his arms. 'Bang ... bang ... bang, good!'

To force the point home he checked the chamber on his weapon and squeezed off three staggered, aimed rounds towards the jungle.

'Okay?'

He got nods in return and slapped them on the back before moving on to the next panicking soldier. This one understood English, negating the need for sign language, and Grant took a moment to catch his breath.

As he gulped the cordite-filled air he felt something wasn't quite right.

Images of his previous encounter with Abdul Mansour flooded his mind, and he knew what the problem was. He got on the radio.

'Colonel, who's manning the front gate?'

'No-one! What you see is all we got. Most of the locals live off base and one of the first buildings to be hit was the accommodation block housing the National Guard. Barely ten people made it out.'

He was astounded that the Filipino troops were not on base with an attack imminent but this wasn't the time to discuss it. 'It's a feint. Mansour doesn't attack head-on. He draws your resources and exploits the weak points.'

A moment of silence, followed by, 'I'll send someone back there.'

'I'll go,' Grant replied, and he grabbed the soldier he had been sheltering with.

'Come on!'

Together they ran across the open ground towards the laundry building. From there it was a left turn to the main gate fifty yards away, but something caught Grant's attention as he peered around the corner. It wasn't coming from the gate, but rather from behind him. He turned in time to see the outline of a pickup truck blazing down the runway, headlights out but a stream of fire erupting from the rear of the vehicle. The accompanying buzz-saw sound told him what was approaching.

'Colonel, mini-gun!' he screamed into the radio as the lance of fire devastated wooden buildings and shredded the wire fence, but Dog had already seen and heard the danger and the net was suddenly alive with his own warnings to get the fuck down.

The truck on the airstrip continued to rain havoc on the camp, puncturing the fuel tank of a jeep and killing the two soldiers who were taking cover behind it. With those deaths they were down to a couple of dozen men, and the number was falling fast as more mortar rounds found their target. From the truck an RPG round shot into the compound and took out the command building, sending flames high into the sky.

Grant got the pickup in his sights but held fire as the truck moved closer and was illuminated by the fires burning all around him. A plank of wood rose from behind the cab and he could see a figure strapped to it. He couldn't see the face but the white skin and fair hair told him it was certainly not a local, which meant it was one of their prisoners, and only one of them had short, fair hair. He quickly got on the radio.

'Colonel, they have one of their hostages tied to the truck.' As an afterthought he added, 'His name is Eddie Halton and he's American.'

Dog began barking the order to cease fire but the local soldiers were in a shooting frenzy, finally having a target they could see. Rounds peppered the truck, puncturing one of the tyres and sending it fishtailing for a moment before the driver got it back under control. It sped down the runway and out of sight, hidden by the airport terminal building. The respite didn't last long as it did a one-eighty and began the return journey, the Dillon spewing fifty rounds a second into the base.

With one tyre shot out it was a job to control the vehicle as it reached fifty miles per hour, but when both wheels on the passenger side were rendered useless by incoming fire it began to slow and yaw like an aeroplane fighting a side wind. The driver tried his best to keep it straight. His efforts ended when a bullet punched through the side window and continued through his neck, entering three inches below the right ear and exiting the other side, destroying his larynx on the way through. He choked to death on his own blood before the vehicle came to a halt.

The two terrorists in the back continued the assault on the camp. One was preparing the second of six RPG-27s while the one manning the Dillon kept his finger on the trigger, despite the warnings he had received from Nabil. At fifty rounds per second, the 4400 bullets in the belt-fed magazine would be exhausted within ninety seconds of continuous fire. Nabil's instructions were to fire short bursts of around three to four seconds to make sure the ammunition lasted the entire assault, but in the heat of battle it was easy to forget such things. Eight seconds after the pickup rolled to a stop, the belt feed relinquished its last round. As it did, the RPG round darted towards the mess hall, blowing a huge hole in the side of the building.

The hostage strapped to the back of the cab was doing nothing to deter retaliatory fire, so the terrorists grabbed two of the single-shot RPGs apiece and jumped over the side of the cargo bed. They headed away from the base, sprinting over the grass towards the chain link fence separating the runway from Junk Town. They both threw their weapons over the top of the fence and began the ascent, but as they climbed one was hit in the small of the back and he lost his grip, dropping several feet before landing in a screaming heap. The other, feeling the bullets whizzing through the air around him, scrambled up the fence and launched himself over the barbed wire atop it.

Without stopping to check on his friend he picked up two RPGs and dashed into the middle of the town, just as Sonny and the two Americans approached it from the left.

From the cover of a food kiosk, Keane surveyed the entrance to Junk Town. Not the official name, it was so called because each dwelling was made from whatever material the inhabitants could find. Walls were made from reclaimed bricks and stone, while the majority of roofs were constructed from corrugated iron. A few had plastic roofs, while some had nothing more than sheets of polyethylene to protect the occupants from the elements.

Two armed men stood at the mouth of the alley leading into the dark village, their rifles hanging loosely in their hands. One was acting as spotter for the concealed mortar teams while the other simply stood and admired the fireworks display emanating from the base.

Keane turned to the others and let them know what they were facing. Sonny swapped places and gauged the distance to the targets and the ground to be covered. Seeing nothing to hinder the takedown, he turned and indicated that he would clear the way using his silenced MP5SD. He got nods in return, pushed the stock of his rifle into his shoulder and broke cover at a crouch.

He approached from their three o'clock and got to within twenty-five yards before they spotted him. As they brought their guns up he straightened and double-tapped them both before they even had a chance to get a shot off. Keane—peering around the corner ready to offer covering fire if things went noisy—saw the men drop and signalled Harrison to follow him. They trotted over and helped drag the bodies out of sight, and once again Sonny took the lead as they headed into the maze of makeshift streets.

The attack on the base had brought the population out of their houses, presenting Sonny with a host of false targets. Fortunately for Sonny, they had about enough to spend on clothing as they did on accommodation, and to a man they wore little more than flip-flops and shorts, with T-shirts for the women. He motioned them aside as he passed, the barrel of his MP5 flicking left and right as he searched for anyone carrying anything more threatening than a penknife.

Sonny heard the familiar *WHOOMP!* as another mortar shell shot into the sky and the sound told him the launcher was close. Ten yards ahead he saw a side street open up and motioned towards it. The smell of rotting food and untreated sewage assaulted his nostrils but his focus was on what lay around the corner. As he approached, a figure appeared carrying a rifle and Sonny immediately got a couple of rounds off. The first missed by a gnat's hair but the second caught the target on the forehead, grazing the skin and ricocheting off the bone beneath. A third round found its mark and the figure crumpled, but not before managing to shout a warning.

'Shit!' Sonny cursed. The last thing he need was the situation to go loud with so many bystanders around.

He rushed to the corner and sneaked a peek, just in time to see the mortar team grabbing their rifles. He hit the first with a double-tap but the second was quicker to his weapon and returned fire, causing Sonny to retreat back around the corner. The firing stopped and he counted to five before sticking a quarter of his head out, but the target had gone.

'One went this way,' he told Keane. 'You two go straight on, see if you can cut him off.'

The two Americans continued down the main alley while Sonny followed the fleeing terrorist. The side street ran for seven yards before turning right, and the mortar had been set up at the corner. He glanced around but saw no-one except a woman consoling a young girl.

The unmistakeable chatter of M16s could be heard a couple of streets away, which told him that Keane and Harrison must have found the target. He followed the sound, stepping round the mother and child and on to the next corner where he once again stopped to clear the turn. He saw his quarry disappear around the next corner, rejoining the main thoroughfare and following in the footsteps of his new team mates. Sonny sprinted after him, knowing that he had to catch up before the shooter got on their six.

Training told him that he should stop at the junction and clear it, but with fellow soldiers in danger he took the risk and barrelled around it, a move which saved his life. The target was standing in wait with his rifle pointed at the corner, ready to destroy any face that appeared. As Sonny exited the side street the rifle spat, but the man behind the trigger wasn't expecting a fast-moving target and his reactions were a little slow, the bullet flying harmlessly wide.

Sonny's training gave him the edge in the encounter. Still moving at speed, he brought his weapon up and put two rounds into centre mass. The man fell instantly and Sonny stopped, took a few steps towards him and put another round through his forehead to make sure the threat was fully neutralised.

From further down the alley he heard yet more gunfire and headed towards it, taking a lot more care when he got to any side streets. With bullets flying just outside their front doors the locals had retreated to the relative safety of their ersatz homes and he had the street to himself, so when the rifle appeared from his right he spotted it instantly.

Getting a bead on the target, he took up the tension on the trigger. Another ounce of pressure and the rifle would spit once more; he just had to wait for a face to follow the gun into the open. A second later he got his wish and a lesser man would have pulled the trigger under the circumstances, but Sonny had no equal when it came to distinguishing friend from foe in high-pressure situations. He dropped the barrel and drew in a foetid breath.

'I heard shots,' he said.

'We took out another mortar team two streets over,' Harrison told him. 'We carried on to the other end of the town. It's clear.'

Sonny told Keane to stay put and asked Harrison to follow him.

'There's a couple of boxes of mortar rounds back here,' he explained as they jogged back to the initial contact point. 'Let's put them to good use.'

They retrieved the ammunition and lugged it back to where Keane was waiting, his M16 pointing into the air and trying his very best—and failing—to look like the archetypal US Army poster boy.

When the figure emerged from a side street ten yards behind Keane, time slowed for Sonny. He saw the weapon in the man's hand and immediately went for his own gun, at the same time shouting a warning. He wasn't about to drop the box of live shells he was carrying and lost a second and a half placing it on the ground. By this time the RPG was almost on the target's shoulder and Sonny stood, grabbing the MP5 which was resting on top of the box and bringing it up in one smooth motion. His first round left the barrel before he'd even pulled the stock of the rifle into his shoulder and flew a couple of inches wide. The next hit the mark but didn't take the man down, the bullet shattering his left collarbone and throwing him off balance. Another squeeze of the trigger and Sonny expected the man to hit the deck, but the firing pin fell on an empty chamber.

Instinctively he reached for the spare magazine, even though he knew he wouldn't have time to load it. He had just removed it from his pocket when the shot came.

With the main threat from the mini-gun on the runway over, Grant realised that there was no more fire coming from the tree line, and the mortars had also stopped. Just as it looked like the attack might be over a blast of heat hit him in the back and sent him sprawling. He looked up to see the main gate hanging from its hinges and approaching fast was a second pickup. It crashed through the twisted metal and came at him on a collision course but he managed to roll himself up against the side of a building just as it sped past. The Filipino soldier had less luck, the truck running over his left leg and snapping it like a twig. His screams of agony were cut short when the gunner in the rear opened up with the Dillon, cutting him in half.

Grant snatched up his rifle but held his fire when he saw that once again there was a hostage strapped to the back of the cab. His heart skipped a beat as he thought it might be Vick, but as the truck passed into the light cast by the numerous fires he could see that the human shield was male, which meant it had to be Moore.

The truck had entered the main square and was driving in a counter-clockwise circle, the gunner and his companion in the back letting loose with all they had. Two soldiers sought cover by diving through a hole in the building's wall but the Dillon followed them and sliced through the thin wood as if it were tissue paper. An RPG round followed for good measure, destroying more of the wall and bringing the roof crashing in. Another RPG round was quick to follow, this one completely destroying the guardhouse.

With the enemy in the tree line forgotten, the Filipino soldiers turned their attention to the truck. Grant knew it was only a matter of time before Moore was hit, so he had to neutralise the threat. His main concern was that the guy behind the Dillon was standing just inches from Moore, and with the vehicle constantly moving and jolting it was not going to be an easy shot.

Decision made, he went for the truck's wheels and engine block, emptying a whole magazine into the front of the vehicle as it swung its nose towards him. The tyre on the passenger side immediately went flat but it did little to kill the speed. The truck continued on its course, showing its back end to Grant, and he went for the rear tyres, puncturing them both. In the back of the truck his actions hadn't gone unnoticed, and an RPG with Grant's name on it was thrown over the terrorist's shoulder. He had his finger on the trigger when Dog took him out with a single, clean head shot.

With his steering becoming erratic, Nabil Shah knew that it wouldn't be long before he became a sitting duck. He gunned the engine and headed for the gate but found Grant standing in his way, inserting a fresh magazine into his rifle. This was the man Abdul had been so concerned about, and killing him was the least he could do for his master. Foot hard to the floor, he drove straight at Grant in the hope of knocking him down as he made his exit.

He didn't get within five yards.

Grant walked the line of bullets from the bottom of the windscreen to the top, shattering the glass and almost splitting the driver down the middle. The truck veered wildly and buried itself in the remains of a shower block, slamming the gunner against the back of the cab where he slumped onto the deck of the cargo bay.

Grant ran over to finish the gunner off from close range but when he pointed the rifle over the side wall he saw just the terrorist Dog had taken down. Before he had time to wonder where the gunner was he took a punch to the right temple that floored him. It felt like he'd been hit by a grizzly bear, and when he managed to look up his hazy vision told him he wasn't far wrong.

When the pickup had hit the wall, Ox had jumped over the other side and snuck around the back of the vehicle. He now stood next to Grant and was reaching down for the M16 he had dropped.

Groggy, Grant pulled his knees up and kicked Ox square in the chest, knocking him backwards. He rolled onto his side to reach for the weapon but Ox was on him quickly and stamped on his arm. He brought his other foot crashing down on Grant's face, smashing his nose. With blood pouring down his face and tears in his eyes Grant struggled to get his act together. He knew that if he didn't move quickly he would be dead in moments, and any action was much better than inaction.

He got up on one knee and launched himself at the blurry figure in front of him, managing to get both hands around Ox's waist. He pumped his legs and lifted with all the strength he could muster, hoping to catch the man off balance, but Ox grabbed his wrists and easily managed to pull him off. A knee in the face followed and Grant collapsed, spent. He was simply too dazed to put up any more resistance and Ox could see it. He picked up the rifle and aimed it at Grant's head, no emotion on his face whatsoever. A volley of fire followed, and Grant's face was covered with blood.

It had come from Ox's chest, ripped open as Len put half a dozen rounds through his spine. Smart put his hand out and helped Grant to his feet.

'Can you still handle a weapon in that state?'

Grant wiped the blood—both his and Ox's—from his face and assured him he could. With the pickup destroyed the firing from the tree line had recommenced, pinning down the few remaining defenders. It wasn't long before he heard the faint sound of a mortar shell leaving the tube and he braced for the impact, but the explosion came from the tree line. Round after round crept along the edge of the jungle, with a couple of RPGs adding to the pyrotechnic display. As a result, the incoming fire petered out, giving Grant time to take stock of the situation.

Less than a dozen men were left standing in the camp, with scores of dead littering the area. Fires burned in the majority of the buildings and not a single vehicle was left serviceable.

While others began tending to the wounded, Grant gingerly helped Moore down from the pickup. He had suffered several gunshot wounds and was in shit state, but none of the injuries seemed life-threatening. A couple of bullets had passed straight through his right arm without hitting bone but one had lodged in his right femur.

'Lie still,' Grant said. 'We'll get you to a hospital as soon as possible.'

'Is E-Eddie ... o-o-okay?' Moore asked, his breath staggered as shock set in and adrenalin pumped through his body.

Grant got up and saw a couple of soldiers at the pickup on the runway. The way they cut his bindings and caught him as he collapsed like a sack of potatoes told him the worst. There was no way to sugar coat it.

'Sorry Robert ... '

Moore closed his eyes, taking in the news. After a few moments they flashed open and he grabbed Grant's arm.

'Abu Sa ... Sayyaf,' he stammered. 'They ha ... have more hos ... hostages. Kids.'

A Filipino joined them and administered morphine, then went to work with his supply of bandages taken from the remains of the medical unit. They applied tourniquets and once Moore was stable Grant left him in the soldier's care.

He found Dog surveying the grisly scene in the accommodation block.

'Why the hell did you let the soldiers go off base when you knew we were about to face an attack?'

'It wasn't my call,' Dog said. 'I shared your intel with the General but he dismissed it. He said Abu Sayyaf are cowards and wouldn't dare attack his base.'

Grant was about to comment on the typical officer arrogance but thought it best not to offend the Colonel. He felt a hand on his shoulder and found Sonny standing next to him.

'Damn, these boys are quick on the draw!'

'We cowboys have a reputation to keep up,' Harrison beamed.

'There I was staring down the launcher of an RPG with my dick in my hand when Harrison whips out his SIG P226 and puts a bullet between the man's eyes from twenty-five yards.' He patted his new best friend on the back. 'We gave them a taste of their own mortars and sent them packing.'

Len joined them and interrupted the back-slapping session. 'We gotta go.'

Grant looked at Dog. 'Colonel?'

Dog shifted his focus from the dead to those who had survived. Some went about their work like automatons while others just stood and stared at the carnage, the shock of battle still to sink in. There was no celebrating the fact that they had managed to repel the attack; just the realisation that they'd evaded death's reach by the narrowest of margins.

'You guys saved a lot of lives today,' he finally said. 'Go. Get as far away as you can.'

'What will you say when they arrive to pick us up?'

'I'll tell them you're missing, presumed dead.'

Grant thanked him, but decided to push his luck further. 'We could do with some gear.'

'What do you need?'

With daylight only a few hours away there wasn't time to get the equipment Sonny and Len had stashed at the LUP. He gave Dog a list, including handguns, knives, ammo, three sets of NVGs and some DPMs to replace his jeans and filthy *sando*.

'That tells me you're not planning to leave the island,' Dog said, letting his expression tell Grant what he thought of the idea.

Grant didn't try to deny it. 'How do you think the General is going to react when he gets here to find his base has been destroyed? Colonel, you know him a lot better than I do, but would I be far wrong if I said he'll want to launch a retaliatory strike within the next twenty-four hours?'

Grant took the lack of response as a Yes. 'They still have a female British hostage, and Moore told me they are also holding some kids. If the local troops go in, they will all be in real danger and you know it.'

Dog indeed knew. No matter how much training he provided to the local troops it was all forgotten the moment they got a sniff of the enemy. The hostages would be stuck in the middle of indiscriminate fire with no way to protect themselves, and casualties would be a certainty.

'We got news of a raid at a small school late yesterday evening. The nun and a guard were killed and nine kids were snatched.' A father himself, Dog couldn't bear to think what they were going through. He certainly couldn't let Callinag go in with all guns blazing.

'What's your plan?'

'Short version? Rescue the hostages and kill any fucker who tries to stop us. We'll work the rest of the details out on the way.'

That brought a brief smile from Dog, but it was tempered by the thought of just three men—no matter how well trained—going up against a camp full of Abu Sayyaf. Sure, they'd taken losses tonight, but there was no way of telling how many. There could still be upwards of a hundred and fifty of them dug in, and with the advantage of the high ground, too.

If his team hadn't been handed a non-combatant role as part of Operation Freedom Eagle, if they had been allowed to do things their own way, he knew he wouldn't be staring at a pile of bodies right now. He also knew he wouldn't get authorisation to launch a rescue mission of his own, even if he did paint it as an attempt to capture Abdul Mansour, and SOCPAC wouldn't let him interfere with any action Callinag decided to take.

Still, there was more than one way to circumvent direct orders. He called his entire team and they were standing before him within a minute. He introduced them to the trio. Garcia, Harrison and Keane they already knew. Evans and Shaw rounded off the SAD complement.

'You guys up for a hunt?' Dog asked his men quietly.

Their reaction was exactly what he expected, every one of them thrilled at the prospect of a proper mission for a change. He spelled out his idea.

'Keane, take these three and get them kitted out with whatever they need. Once they're geared up tell them how to get to the trail, then come running three minutes later to tell me they escaped. I'll order the five of you to go after them. We'll do it nice and loud so it squares things with Callinag when he asks where my team is.'

Nods all round.

'Meet up at the mouth of the trail and Grant will give you the details of the mission. He's been inside the camp, so listen to what he says.'

His men indicated that they had no problem with that directive.

'They have kids in there,' Dog said. 'They are the priority. Other hostages second, Abdul Mansour third.'

The thought of a group of kids in the middle of a firefight cooled their bravado a little, if anything making their mission that much more critical.

'What about afterwards?' Evans asked. 'I mean, what about these guys?'

Dog considered it for a moment. 'You didn't find them. You were looking for them and came across the camp where you were fired upon. You're allowed to use deadly force in self defence, so that's how we'll report it.'

No-one had any questions, so Keane led the trio to the armoury to grab the equipment they needed. At least a couple of shells had hit the building but fortunately none of the ammunition had taken a direct hit. Grant selected a box of 9 mm rounds for the Heckler & Koch machine guns as well as two boxes of 5.56 mm for those using the M16s. After picking a SIG P226 for himself he told the others to look for smoke and fragmentation grenades, which they found in a locked cabinet. He also spotted a box of flares and some grenades for the under-slung M203s. He helped himself to a few of each.

'What about knives?' Grant asked.

'We'll have to scavenge for the rest, including your fatigues,' Keane told him. He led them to the SAD hut which was separate from the National Guard accommodation. It too had sustained damage, but Keane was able to find a spare set of clothes for Grant in Harrison's locker. He also raided the foot lockers and found a pair of boots for Grant and two knives, which he gave to Len and Sonny.

'Shit!'

Keane's NVGs had been damaged in the raid, the delicate equipment not being able to stand up to the pounding they'd taken. Another pair was completely smashed but they found two sets which were functioning.

Grant finished changing and began jotting down a note on a small piece of paper.

'The trail begins around five hundred metres from the camp,' Keane told them. 'Take a right out of the gate and you'll see it on your right-hand side. It's nothing more than a dirt track, so keep your eyes peeled. Once you get into the trees, go on for another fifty metres and we'll meet you there soon.'

Grant handed him the slip of paper and asked him to pass it to the Colonel, then the trio grabbed their gear and jogged up the road, finding the track near where Keane had said it would be. They followed it into the outer reaches of the jungle and occupied their time by filling their magazines with the ammunition they'd brought along.

'I thought we were going to be heading back to warn Carl and Jeff,' Len said, concerned that his friends in the UK were still in danger and unaware of it.

'I asked the Colonel to call Timmy Hughes in Singapore,' Grant said. 'He'll ask Timmy to give the boys the heads-up and expect a call from us. If we make it out of here, that is.'

'Which brings me on to my next question,' Len said. 'Why exactly are we here? Is it the kids, Abdul Mansour, or the girl?'

Grant had known these two men for too long—and had been through too much with them—to even think about lying. As a father who had lost his own son at a tender age, he couldn't in all conscience sit back and let those kids go through a major attack. He also blamed Mansour for putting him in this position in the first place. Without his interference, Grant would be a free man in his own country rather than a fugitive. Without a doubt, though, the main driving force was Vick Phillips, and he admitted as much.

'Do you still want to tag along?' he asked them.

'Do bears shit themselves when they see me in the woods? Of course I'm coming along!'

Sonny also agreed, and they continued their preparation for another fifteen minutes until they caught sight of the American team approaching.

'Sorry we're late,' Harrison said in his Texas drawl. 'The General turned up just as we were ready to leave. He brought a shit-storm along for good measure.'

'Why?' Grant asked. 'He was told that an attack was imminent and he ignored the warning. Even if you don't think a threat is credible, you prepare for it. You don't order all of your troops off base.'

'Yeah, it's the Colonel's problem now,' Len said.

'It will soon be our problem,' Keane said. 'Callinag wants to hit them at first light, which is why he wasn't happy with us disappearing like we did.'

'How long does that give us?' Sonny asked, and was told they had a little over four hours.

'There must be about a hundred Abu Sayyaf hightailing it back to their camp right now,' Harrison said. 'If we can get on their tail we should be able to take a few out.'

'We could,' Len agreed, 'but that might alert them to our presence. I say we let them get back, let the adrenalin wear off and take them while they sleep.'

Jones asked what they would do if they weren't in a hurry to get back and a quick discussion on possible scenarios took place. Grant asked for a map of the area and wanted to know the likely route Abu Sayyaf would take during their retreat.

'If we stay on this track, are we likely to run into them?' he asked.

'Not for some time, if they take the shortest way home,' Garcia told him, indicating the markings on his map. 'There is a network of tracks throughout the area, and they are most likely to follow this route.'

He traced a line from the airstrip to the top of Hill 178, and then drew another from their current location to the same destination point.

'We remain roughly seven hundred metres from them until we get to this point.' He indicated a spot a kilometre from the terrorist camp, and Grant could see the two tracks converging.

'I say we get a sprint on and get there first. The fewer people in the camp, the better our chances of securing the hostages.'

With everyone in agreement they divided up the ammunition, checked their pockets and pouches to make sure they didn't rattle as they ran, and then set off at a shade over jogging pace. The dirt track soon gave way to denser jungle and what was once a clear path became nothing more than a narrow channel through the undergrowth. The sound of fixed-wing fighters could be heard overhead and Grant hoped they'd been informed about the hostages plus the fact that friendly forces were in the area. If they hadn't, it could turn very hot, very quickly.

The Americans, being familiar with the route, each took a turn on point, remaining a hundred yards ahead of the others. They would stop at regular intervals to switch point man and listen for any sign of the enemy, but the first leg of their journey went without incident.

After an hour and a half they reached the spot where they would begin to close on the enemy and Grant suggested a two-man patrol take the NVGs and scout the area ahead. While they did, he and the others took the opportunity to catch their breath. Although he'd been fit for most of his life, a ninety-minute run through the jungle in oppressive heat was taxing enough for anyone, and he was glad to see he wasn't the only one suffering.

He brushed aside some dead leaves and used a stick to draw in the soft earth.

'As I remember it, the camp is circular, roughly seventy yards across. The perimeter is lined with trees and there are more trees dotted throughout which they use to rig their hammocks. The hostages were being held over here but that may have changed.

'At the back of the camp the hill continues on to the summit, so we should be able to approach from these three sides.' He used the stick to indicate possible entry routes.

Sonny and Shaw returned after twenty minutes, and the news was both good and bad.

'There isn't a lot of sound coming from the area, which suggests they aren't back yet, but those who stayed behind are nicely dug in. There's a track leading up to the camp and we saw movement from a couple of foxholes either side of it. If we go in that way we'll be torn apart.'

'We could try skirting to the left or right of the track and get to the camp that way,' Len said, but Sonny explained that they had tried that and spotted another foxhole not far from the first.

'My bet is that they have a ring all the way around the camp,' he said, although he admitted that they hadn't had time to verify it.

'Are they two up in each hole?'

'It looks like just one,' Shaw said. 'I would have expected two, but maybe they sent the majority of their people on the assault.'

Grant was acutely aware that time was short, and they had to make a decision.

'We can't hang around forever. Their wounded might be slowing them up but that doesn't mean we have all night. I say we clear those two holes, go straight up the middle and surprise the hell out of anyone still in the camp.'

He waited for dissenters but there were none.

'Okay. Sonny, how close do you think you can get to them?'

'We can get to within fifty yards easily. Any closer and we risk detection.'

Grant asked who was comfortable with a head shot from that distance and two of the Americans declared it an easy takedown.

'Ever use the MP5 before?' he asked them. They had in fact used the naval variant, so they were given the task of clearing the way.

'Once the track is open I need you to get as close to the camp as possible and report numbers and locations. We'll be right behind you and when we know where the X-rays are we split into two-man teams.'

He paired everyone up, with Len and Sonny working together while he would accompany Evans.

'We need to keep this as quiet as possible, otherwise we'll have them crawling out of their holes and they'll be coming at us from all sides. Once it goes noisy get those NVGs off straight away because I'll be popping flares. Hopefully it won't come to that. I'd much rather cure their SBA while they're sleeping.'

'SBA?' Harrison asked, puzzled.

Sonny smiled. 'Still Being Alive.'

Shaw and Garcia took the NVGs and silenced weapons and made their way to their positions. The area ahead of them was bathed in a sea of light-green twilight as the optical core of the NVGs magnified the light from the barely visible quarter moon and allowed them to see distinct shapes impossible to distinguish with the naked eye.

'When you get into position and have a target, send me two clicks,' Garcia whispered. 'I'll respond with the same when I'm eyes-on.'

They split up, one either side of the dirt track leading up to the plateau. On their bellies they crawled towards their targets, ever mindful to clear away any fallen twigs or dry leaves that could create noise and give their location away. This cautious approach meant it was six minutes before they were on target.

Shaw brought up his weapon and trained it on the figure beneath the canopy and sent the signal to his sergeant, getting two clicks in reply. There wasn't a lot to aim at through the eight-inch gap, especially as he could only see the top half of the head, but as a former marine he knew how to shoot. All marines needed to attain the rank of marksman, the lowest grade required to exit initial training. Shaw had not only beaten the minimum required score but also exceeded that needed to earn the sharpshooter badge, his skills giving him the honour of being called an expert. He saw the current shot, a four-inch target from fifty metres, about as difficult as hitting a buffalo's ass with a banjo, especially as the fool thought it a brilliant idea to smoke while on lookout. He was lit up like a Christmas tree, just inviting a bullet.

Shaw was happy to oblige.

Five seconds later his night sights showed a puff of green exit the back of the head and he signalled the kill to Garcia, who responded in kind a few seconds later. They waited to see if the alarm had been raised but they heard nothing to suggest they had given the game away.

'Clear,' Garcia said into his comms unit, and the others moved up cautiously to join them. By the time Grant arrived Shaw was already approaching the camp. Keeping his head just below the edge of the plateau he manoeuvred towards a tree and used it to hide half of his profile as he slowly rose to view the scene. He took six seconds to take in the details before slowly drawing back, making no sudden movements likely to bring him to anyone's attention.

Garcia watched as Shaw relayed the details and as he had the only other pair of NVGs he translated the signals for the others. With the camp being circular, Shaw represented positions analogous to a clock face.

'Hostages are at the four o'clock, ten metres in, two guards on them. Five more in the centre of the camp, talking around a fire. Between eight and ten o'clock there are seven or eight sleeping. Three sleeping at one o'clock, and four more sleeping at three o'clock.

'There's a mini-gun fifteen metres in, and it's pointing towards the track, two up.'

'Any sign of Mansour?' Grant asked. Garcia relayed the question over the net but the response from Shaw was a shrug of the shoulders.

Twenty-four targets didn't represent a massive force, but with almost half of them awake it was going to get noisy a lot earlier than Grant wanted. The obvious first targets were the guards on the hostages and the two manning the Dillon, a thought he shared with the others.

'Agreed,' Garcia said. He hit the throat mike so that Shaw could hear his instructions. 'I'll take the two on the hostages and Shaw can take out the mini-gun. After that we both go for the five in the middle. If we can take them down without waking the others we'll clear the rest. If at any time the alert goes out, the rest of you pick your targets.

'Grant and Evans, you go right. Baines and Smart go left. I'll take Harrison down the centre along with Keane and Shaw.

'Any questions?'

There were none, just two clicks from Shaw to acknowledge the instructions.

'Good luck, gentlemen.'

Chapter Thirteen

Friday 20 April 2012

The overriding principle behind any plan is KISS: Keep It Simple, Stupid! That was what Grant had always been taught, and what they were about to attempt was as simple as they could make it, under the circumstances. As with any plan, there was always the unexpected that simply couldn't be factored in, and that was why the ability to adapt instantly often meant the difference between death and survival.

Grant was less than ten seconds into his latest mission when it all went to shit, and that ability kicked in.

Just as they entered the camp, a guard left his defensive position and tracked along the side of the hill in search of a cigarette from his friend in the adjacent hole. Finding him with a bullet in the forehead, he shouted a warning that brought everyone to their feet.

With their cover blown, Shaw kicked off the assault, taking out the two men who were readying the mini-gun. As he did so, Garcia dispatched one of the men guarding the hostages, but the other was quicker to the danger and managed to duck down behind the prisoners. He raised his weapon and fired over the heads of the children in the direction of the attackers, spraying bullets in a sweeping arc.

Grant shouted his own warning to those wearing the NVGs and popped one of the flares, bathing the scene in an artificial light which cast deep shadows and gave the camp an eerie feeling. With one eye closed to protect his own night vision he ran to the right, firing as he went. He managed one hit but the element of surprise was lost and their targets had gone to ground.

He got to the tree line and popped a smoke grenade, lobbing it beyond the group of hostages, then continued his run to get round the back of them. The remaining guard was lying on his back and switching out magazines when Grant got to him, and he smashed the butt of his rifle into his face, knocking the fight out of him. Grant drew his pistol, held it to the man's forehead and grabbed him around the throat.

'Where is Mansour?' He screamed into the bloodied face. The reply was muted but he understood the single word: '*Wala*'.

Mansour was gone.

Grant put a round between the man's eyes.

'Tom!'

Vick was on her feet and picking her way through the crowd of children who were cowering on the ground, and the sight of her made Grant hesitate for a second. Despite her being his main reason for taking part in the assault he was caught off guard and forgot himself for a brief moment. It was only the sensation of a bullet whizzing past his head that shook him out of his reverie.

'Get down!' he shouted, spinning towards the trees. Before the flare gave up the last of its light he saw figures climbing the hill towards the camp, firing as they advanced. Evans was already engaging them and Grant joined in, pinning them down. He grabbed a fragmentation grenade and lobbed it towards them but instead of landing and exploding it ricocheted off a rock and detonated harmlessly beyond them. Evans had more luck with his

M203. He aimed at the ground to the right of a tree and the resulting blast dismembered the man standing behind it.

'We need to clear a path and get these kids out of here,' Grant said into his mike. It wasn't quite a shout but it conveyed the urgency of the moment. He turned and sent another flare rocketing towards the leafy canopy and as he did he saw a figure approaching through the bank of smoke. The Dillon, still on its tripod, was cradled in his right arm, and he was dragging the belt-fed magazine behind him. Grant brought up his rifle and was a millisecond away from dropping him when the smoke parted and he made out Harrison's features.

With a huge grin that said: 'I always wanted one of these,' he stopped at the top of the slope and let rip into the jungle. Smaller trees disintegrated as he swept the muzzle of the weapon from side to side, and the incoming fire stopped abruptly as the attackers were cut down.

'We have the kids and an exit,' Grant said over the net. 'Everyone, on me!'

He screamed for the adults and children to get down the hill, he and Evans urging them along with helpful shoves; in the heat of battle, there just wasn't time for niceties.

On the other side of the camp Len and Sonny were being pinned down by fire from in front and from their left. Keane eased the pressure with a couple of well-aimed M203 rounds and was readying a third when a bullet caught him in the chest and he fell backwards, his gun slipping from his dead hands.

'Keane is down!' Shaw shouted, pouring more fire onto the enemy. A couple of grenades followed and the response from the Filipinos dwindled, allowing them all the opportunity to crab their way over to Grant. More smoke grenades were thrown to mask their retreat and soon the only gunfire came from the few remaining Abu Sayyaf, shooting blindly into the haze in the futile hope of hitting targets long since out of their line of sight.

Vick had assumed the lead and was guiding the other hostages down the hill when Grant screamed for her to stop. He had come across one of the defensive positions and the plastic triggers for the Claymore mines were all too familiar. He called Sonny over.

'Trace this to the mine and watch out for trip wires. We'll take them with us, just in case.'

They slowly gathered the wire in as they walked down the hill, keeping a keen eye out for signs that they were rigged to explode automatically.

Shaw and Garcia had remained near the top of the hill and as a couple of faces peered over the edge they did nothing, in the hope of sucking more targets into their sights. Unfortunately one of the terrorists raised his weapon with the aim of hitting a fleeing figure and both men were forced to open up, cutting him down. They got a barrage of incoming fire in return. The shooters were lying flat inside the camp while extending their arms over the edge and spraying lead indiscriminately. Fortunately their aim was too high to endanger life and Shaw sent a fragmentation grenade arcing into their midst in order to silence them.

The explosion brought an end to the immediate battle.

Grant and Sonny reached their mines without killing themselves or anyone else and they deactivated their respective devices.

'Take point,' Grant said to Garcia as he joined up with them. 'We need to get these kids out of here before the others turn up.' He took a moment to get his bearings. 'They'll be coming from the north, so we need to head west. Are there any towns that way?'

'No, there's nothing. We'll have to track west and head north after a couple of clicks. That'll bring us out near the airport and we should be able to avoid any contact.'

'Okay, you lead the way.' Grant called the men together and allocated their positions. 'Shaw, you stay on our right flank and keep your eyes peeled. Harrison, Evans, take the rear and cover our retreat with the mini-gun. The rest of us will help keep the kids quiet.'

The adult hostages were having trouble with this as most of them were as frightened as the children, but with Grant, Sonny and Len there were now almost enough adults to take care of one child each. The men were assigned to the larger children, leaving the smaller ones for the women just in case they had to carry them at any point.

One more adult would have been perfect, but it took at least two people to carry the Dillon along with its magazine and power unit. Even with a quarter of its rounds expended, the entire unit still weighed close to two hundred pounds.

Grant gathered them all together and explained the situation, choosing words he hoped the young ones would understand.

'We're taking you home to your parents now, but there are some bad men looking for us, so we have to be very quiet.'

He was sure the pained expressions on their faces were due to having this ugly foreigner address them, but Vick leaned over and whispered in his ear.

'They're orphans.'

Grant let loose a quiet expletive. 'Okay, then we'll take you back to the orphanage.'

This didn't go down well, either.

'It was run by one woman, Sister Evangelina. She was hacked to death in front of them.'

Of all the battles he'd taken part in, Grant had a feeling this was one he was not going to win.

'You tell them,' he whispered back. 'Just make sure they know to keep quiet.'

Vick had obviously gained their trust during the short time they'd been together. The children nodded, a few smiling, when she explained that they were going to take them somewhere safe and give them some hot food and a soft, comfortable bed.

'But you all have to stay close to your grown-up and do as they say,' she emphasised, 'and be very, very quiet.'

More nods, and she declared them ready to go. Grant sent Garcia on ahead and gave him a two-minute start before leading his charges into the darkness. Daylight was still another two hours away and their progress was slow to begin with. The moon was struggling to penetrate the treetops and what little light got through cast shadows across their path, so they didn't know if their feet were about to fall on shade or a hole in the ground.

Garcia reported in every two minutes, letting everyone know that he was still alive as well as reporting any hazards or obstacles the kids might have trouble with. For their part the children behaved as well as Grant could have hoped, but their first challenge lay just yards ahead.

He heard the river before he saw it. When he reached the bank he saw that it was at least twenty feet across, and although the surface water wasn't racing there was always the undercurrent to consider. Garcia was waiting for him.

'Should be fine for us to cross, but the kids might find it more difficult.'

Grant agreed, and offered a solution. 'Form a chain and help them across?'

'That works for me. I'll send Harrison ten yards downstream, just in case one of them gets away from us.'

They explained the plan to the others, who were much happier to have the help of the soldiers rather than make the crossing by themselves.

Harrison set the mini-gun on its tripod and walked a few yards down the bank, where he eased himself gingerly into the river before wading out towards the centre. By the time he reached the halfway point it was lapping above his navel, which equated to neck-high for the adult Filipino hostages, never mind the children.

Shaw remained in the trees, keeping an eye out, while the other five men entered the water and formed a line from one bank to the other. Grant could feel the undercurrent constantly tugging at his calves and knew it wouldn't be long before they started to cramp up, so he beckoned to the first person.

The Chinese male was the first across, followed by his wife a minute later. One by one they crossed the river until there was just Vick and two of the children remaining.

Shaw's voice came over the radio. 'We've got company.'

'Where and how close?'

'This side of the river, a hundred metres and closing. I see eight ... no, make that twelve.'

Grant knew there wasn't much time before they were spotted, and he had to get the remaining people across. He urged Vick to send the next child over quickly, but his actions told her something was wrong. In a panic, she was a little too forceful with the young girl and rather than guide her into the hands of Grant she virtually pushed her into the river. The girl lost her footing immediately and her head went under the water, reappearing a few feet further downstream.

'Help her!' Vick pleaded to Harrison. Everyone else held their breath, as if doing so might prevent her cry from carrying to the enemy, but Shaw confirmed the worst.

'They heard us,' he said. 'Get them across. I'll cover you.'

He immediately began picking off the targets one by one using the silenced weapon, but as each went down another two seemed to appear from nowhere. With their numbers swelling and their advance quickening, they began returning fire in all directions, still not sure where the attack was coming from. They soon got an idea when Shaw switched to the mini-gun and sent a six second burst in their direction. Over a dozen were killed and the rest hit the jungle floor seeking whatever cover they could find. A few had the nerve to return fire but their vision was limited to a few feet and their bullets flew wildly. Shaw picked up on their muzzle flashes and began picking them off with the Dillon, firing a short burst before shifting his aim and hitting them again, until finally they got the message and held their fire.

Harrison had plucked the girl from the current and carried her over to the far bank where she was reunited with the others. Vick, meanwhile, was shaken by the incident and Grant had to climb out of the river to get the remaining child. After passing her over to Sonny he went back for Vick.

'Come on,' he said, taking hold of her arm. 'This is the last hurdle. Once we're across we'll be home free.'

She followed his lead, refusing to release her grip on his hand until they reached the safety of the opposite bank. Shaw was still pinning the enemy down whenever he saw any sign of movement and Garcia told him to join up with them. Rather than leave the Dillon to the enemy, Shaw first emptied the magazine in their direction before pressing the latch on the safing top cover and opening it, which put the weapon into 'safe' mode. He then extracted a pin from a fragmentation grenade and jammed it between the latch and its housing. The sergeant took up the defence while he navigated his way to the other side, and when the grenade exploded it tore off the latch, rendering the weapon unusable. Grant had calmed Vick down enough to get her to let go of him and was waiting with the Claymores when he climbed up the bank.

'Let's get into the jungle and leave an obvious trail,' he said. 'I'll set the first one up after a hundred yards and the other fifty yards after that.'

They set off once again, this time at a faster pace. When they came to a good spot, Grant stopped and urged the others to continue onwards. Garcia pulled out a device and began punching keys.

'Just marking the position on my GPS,' he said when he saw Grant's quizzical expression. 'If it doesn't get tripped in the next hour we'll come back and disarm it once reinforcements arrive.'

Grant secured one end of the tripwire around the trunk of a tree and pulled it across the path they had created before securing the other end in the trigger mechanism. He then covered the mine itself with detritus from the surrounding area and moved on to set up the next one.

With both traps set they jogged after the others, happy in the knowledge that if they were still being pursued the mines would at least slow their efforts, if not halt them altogether.

After another twenty minutes the first signs of morning broke through the trees, bringing with it a downpour. A muffled explosion from their rear signalled one of the traps being sprung and that told them they had a sizeable lead on those following. Grant saw it as the ideal time to take a short rest and he showed the kids how to catch rainwater in leaves to quench their thirst. It had been a long time since any of them had taken on liquid and he decided to let them drink their fill before moving on again.

Vick was standing a few feet away from him, her face pointing towards the heavens as she enjoyed the impromptu shower. Despite the setting—or perhaps because of it—she struck Grant as the most beautiful creature he'd ever seen, and in that instance he knew he could never bear to let her go. He also knew that it would be unfair, even irresponsible, to drag her into what was undoubtedly going to be a titanic struggle to reclaim his former life.

His thoughts were interrupted when she came over and put a gentle hand on his arm.

'I'm sorry for making all that noise at the river,' she said. 'I just panicked.'

Grant told her not to worry about it. No-one had been hurt and they were almost out of danger. It was a bittersweet thought, as he knew it would mean saying goodbye for the last time.

'I haven't even thanked you for saving our lives,' she said, and kissed him softly on the cheek.

'Come with me.'

The words were out of his mouth before he knew it, and he couldn't tell who was more shocked by them. For the first time in his life his heart had been battling his head, and that simple peck on the cheek had been the clincher.

Vick saw the look of panic on his face and regained her composure before he could retract the request. 'Okay.'

Grant was about to backtrack, to make an excuse for the outburst, when Sonny interrupted and told him that Garcia wanted a word with them. He grabbed his weapon and they walked over to the sergeant, his thoughts still jumbled.

'The Colonel has been in touch. He said that Callinag has sent out the first of his patrols and they should be in the area pretty soon.'

'That's not good,' Grant said. 'If they see us it is going to raise a lot of questions and we can't afford to hang around to answer them.'

'I know, the Colonel explained your situation. I was going to tell you a few minutes ago but I didn't want to interrupt your reunion.' He nodded towards Vick with a knowing smile and Grant wondered if his feelings for her were as obvious to everyone else. Their sly grins confirmed the worst.

'Bollocks to you lot! What else did the Colonel say?'

'Your friend has arranged to pick you up ten miles off the west coast of the island. He'll be there in forty-eight hours.' Garcia read off the coordinates to the remaining Claymore so that Evans could transfer them to his own device before handing his own GPS over to Grant.

'Your rendezvous is the first number in the list,' Garcia said, explaining how the device worked. 'I've named it Timmy so you know which one it is. Just select it from the list and it brings up a map showing your current location and the destination.'

Grant took the device, hit the 'Back' button and saw two other items on the list: Meeting and Sleep. 'What are these?'

Garcia explained that Sleep represented a small cave four miles to the south that they could hide in until they were ready to head out to sea. It was an area of little activity and so the chances of being found were slim. 'The Colonel is making arrangements for a boat to be left at this location,' Garcia said, bringing up the Meeting coordinates. 'It will be delivered at ten tomorrow evening, which will give you roughly six hours to get on station.'

Grant stowed the device in his pocket and thanked them for helping with the rescue.

'You've got a good team here, Sergeant. I'm sorry about Keane.'

There was naturally a professional rivalry between all armed forces units, each believing themselves to be the best. However, deep down it was begrudgingly accepted that the SAS were the true masters of special warfare, and so Garcia recognised the short statement as praise indeed. He too would miss Keane, but like Grant, his years as a professional soldier had prepared him for such events.

'It comes to all of us,' he said philosophically.

Grant asked Sonny and Len to give him a moment while he squared things with Vick. He still couldn't understand why he'd made her the offer, but it was something he couldn't go through with. Vick saw the look on his face as he approached and guessed what was coming.

'Don't you dare try and leave me here,' she warned him. Grant put up his hands to placate her but she was going to have her say, whether he liked it or not.

'You just asked me to come with you!'

'This isn't your fight, Vick.'

'Don't give me that!' she shouted. 'I've been stuck in this jungle for three months and my government did nothing!'

He tried to keep his voice level rather than engage in a shouting match. 'Vick, where I'm going it will be dangerous. I can't ask you to be part of that.'

'Dangerous! What would you call the last few hours? A walk in the park? Tom, I'm coming with you!'

'It won't be the same kind of danger, Vick. Here you know who your enemies are. Back in England you'll have no idea until it is too late.'

'I can handle it,' she said, defiantly.

'Like you did at the river? You nearly cost that child her life and your actions gave away our position to the enemy.'

Vick didn't like the accusation but had to admit that she'd not covered herself in glory. The tension of the last quarter of a year began to bubble to the surface and the thought of endangering the child's life finally broke her resolve. As the tears came Grant placed a gentle hand on her cheek and rubbed them away with his thumb.

'Vick, I love you, but where I'm going—'

'What?'

Grant looked confused, while Vick suddenly perked up. 'What?' he asked in return.

'You said you loved me.'

'No I didn't.'

'Yes you did, Tom Gray! You said "Vick, I love you"!'

As he struggled to rewind the last few seconds in his mind she took advantage of his bewilderment and grabbed his face, planting her lips onto his. He wrapped his arms around her and returned the kiss, his argument for leaving her on the island crumbling with every passing moment.

Sonny walked past and slapped Grant on the shoulder.

'Get a room, guys. Better yet, I know a good cave not far from here ... '

Grant realised that he'd been outflanked and outmanoeuvred, but a part of him knew that he hadn't really been putting up much of a fight.

'I'm serious,' he said as he held her close. 'The next few weeks are going to be tough. It may even be months before this is all over.'

'I don't care. I'm coming with you.'

He slipped an arm around her shoulder and they set off in pursuit of Len and Sonny.

'So what's your plan?' she asked.

'Plan A is to take a shower. After that I want to find the people who are trying to kill me.'

It was Vick's turn to look confused. 'A couple of days ago the government was sending someone to rescue you.' She pointed up the trail towards his friends. 'I take it that was these two. What's changed?'

'It's a long story.'

Vick smiled. 'I've got all night.'

Chapter Fourteen

Friday 20 April 2012

Azhar Al-Asiri finished the *Asr*, or afternoon prayer—the third of five he would perform that day—before picking at a plate of flat bread and *Sajji*, a lightly spiced leg of lamb cooked by roasting it next to an open fire. The food was good, freshly prepared by his 'family' in the home situated in the Pashton Abed district of Quetta, Pakistan.

The people he lived with weren't actually blood relatives, nor was the dwelling a single apartment. Instead it was three apartments connected by hidden doorways, and his family consisted of a daughter, Nyla, and two grandchildren. Nyla was in fact the widow of a martyr who had given his life to the cause, and her two children—the girl, Hifza, and the boy, Mufid—played an integral part in ensuring Al-Asiri remained anonymous.

His accommodation could have been more opulent, but that would have attracted unwanted attention. His preference was to live in simple surroundings, just another face in a city of two million. That wasn't to say he placed all of his trust in this simple ruse. The buildings surrounding him were home to his loyal supporters, and lookouts were posted in a wide radius to give notice of any unwanted visitors. They ranged from the young boys playing football to the old man smoking and drinking coffee outside the café, all keeping an eye out for government troops or foreign snatch squads.

Each of the lookouts carried a simple early-warning device. It was the size of a matchbox and had a button in the middle, which, when pressed three times in rapid succession, would send a signal to Al-Asiri's home. This would allow him time to get down to the cellar where a network of tunnels led to various exfiltration points. By the time his enemies got to his home he could be emerging from one of eight different shafts and be spirited away by his loyal followers.

A glance at his watch told him it was almost time to check for messages. Wary that telephone calls could be traced and Web traffic could be tracked by IP address, Al-Asiri kept no such instruments on the premises. Instead all communications went through a computer in the basement of a jeweller's shop half a mile from his apartment.

The shop had a CCTV system that would be expected in any such establishment, but as well as monitoring the shop and its customers it was used to keep an eye out for uninvited guests.

Access to the rear of the shop was through a metal cage. The employees would use a security card to open the outer door and once inside they would use the same card to release the inner door. The outer door had to be closed before the inner would operate, preventing more than two people entering the room at the same time. The card system also recorded the movement of staff and prevented them sharing a card. If an employee swiped his way into the workshop, his card would not allow anyone else entry until he had swiped his way out again. Once through the cage, the employees then had to negotiate a heavy wooden door which finally granted access to the workshop.

All of this could be explained away as security for the valuable stock, but the real purpose was to deny quick entry to the cellar which lay beneath the workshop floor.

The communications room was constantly manned through-out the day. Each shift lasted twelve hours and the room had everything the occupant required to see them through to the handover: a toilet, and food and water which were replenished four times a day.

It was to this communications centre that Al-Asiri sent his 'grandson', Mufid.

As always, he wrote his message on a small piece of paper, rolled into a tight tube and placed it inside a small plastic recep-tacle similar to a medicine capsule. The boy placed the capsule under his tongue and took a walk to the jeweller's, ready to swallow the evidence if anyone tried to halt his progress.

The trip was uneventful, and ten minutes later he handed the capsule over to his uncle, who disappeared into the back. A few minutes later he returned with an identical capsule which Mufid took back to the apartment.

Al-Asiri read the note before setting fire to it in an ashtray. Two more teams had reported in, making five in total. Only one remained outstanding, Abdul Mansour's, but given his location Al-Asiri didn't expect to hear from him until he was closer to civilisation. It wasn't as if he could simply walk into an Internet café in the middle of the jungle, and Abdul knew better than to make contact via an insecure phone. It was more likely that he would see his handiwork on the news channels before he received a report, and knowing his young general, it would be something spectacular.

He reflected on how far the young man had come in such a short time, and it saddened him that he couldn't quite trust him fully. Mansour had arrived in Pakistan at a tender age and had been quick to show his allegiance, dispatching a captured US soldier with chilling efficiency. The transition from taking part in raids to planning and leading them had been swift, and his execu-tion of the attack on Tom Gray's fortress had been masterful.

However, he still had doubts about someone so young being so capable.

His enemies would love nothing more than to have an agent infiltrate the organisation, and it seemed a little strange that Mansour should arrive on the scene with skills not normally seen in a teenager from a poor area of London. He had since shown himself to be a natural born killer, but according to background reports he had previously been involved in nothing more serious than a few playground fights.

So where did he acquire these skills? That had been the question on his mind for the last two years, and at first he'd suspected that it had been courtesy of the British security services. However, discreet surveillance had shown no signs of any communications with anyone outside the organisation. In fact, all they had seen was a devout Muslim, apparently true and loyal to the cause.

He had approved Mansour's plan to attack Tom Gray as a way of testing his credentials. If the attack had been foiled it may have suggested that Mansour had tipped the security services off and they had baulked at the idea, but he had actually succeeded, killing Gray and denying him the chance to tell the government where his bomb was. That they found it in time was perhaps luck, maybe good police work, but whom had Mansour actually killed? Tom Gray, a terrorist in his own government's eyes; a couple of his associates; and a handful of police officers. Would the British government have allowed that toll in order to protect Mansour's true allegiance?

After all this time he still hadn't come to a conclusion about his young general, but the result of his Asian mission—and more importantly, Mansour's next assignment in the UK—would offer the defining answer.

Farrar had been sitting outside the office for nearly twenty minutes when the door opened and the familiar figure of the Home Secretary stormed out, his face like thunder. Farrar's boss stuck his head out and told him to enter, then offered him the warm seat recently vacated by the Minister.

'You've got a reprieve,' Charles Benson said without preamble. 'It seems our friend Mr Gray is a much more resourceful character than I gave him credit for. The team we sent to collect him has reported him missing.'

Missing? Farrar perked up at that news.

'It seems there was a little altercation with the locals and he managed to escape, along with his two acquaintances.'

'What about a search of the island? They can't have got very far.'

Benson dismissed the idea with a flick of the wrist. 'We haven't got the resources or jurisdiction. The reason I brought you back in is that you've known this man for over a year. You've been through every inch of his file, spoken with him, observed him. What are his intentions?'

Farrar considered his answer carefully. If he admitted to having no idea, his usefulness would immediately evaporate. Better to play the subject-matter expert.

'He's got two things on his mind: the first is revenge; the second is survival. Given the events of last year I'm afraid we cannot discount the former.'

'Last year he had the advantage of anonymity, plus a sound financial footing. Do you really think he'll come after you?'

The question left Farrar under no illusion: the trail stopped with him.

'That's a possibility, but it's a long way home. As you said, he has no money. I also know he hasn't got a passport, and he'll need both to get back to the UK. That gives us plenty of time to set up border protocols across Europe and beyond.

'He will have to seek help from others, and we have a comprehensive list of former acquaintances, from his Army days up to his time as Managing Director of Viking Security Services. I'm confident that anyone he contacts will be on that list.'

'That sounds like it could be a long list. We can't possibly monitor everyone on it,' Benson observed.

'True, but his buddies in Britain aren't going to be a lot of help to him right now. He's going to need someone in the local area and only two people spring to mind. One is in Vietnam, the other in Singapore.'

Benson nodded. 'What of the remaining two, Levine and Campbell? Are plans in place to deal with them?'

'They are. We expect those problems to go away within the next fortnight.'

'Why so long?'

'We have to work to their patterns,' Farrar explained, 'otherwise suspicions will be aroused.'

Benson sat back in his chair and folded his arms. 'Consider this your last chance, James. If this mess isn't cleared up soon you can kiss your career goodbye. We cannot simply blame this on the previous government, no matter how appealing it sounds. I want an end to the whole Tom Gray saga, or you will be the one to take the fall.'

Benson picked up a pen and opened a folder, signalling the end of the meeting. Farrar got up from his chair and let himself out of the office, the threat still clear in his head. As he stepped from the government building into an April shower he knew that failure wouldn't simply mean spending the rest of his life in prison: his very life depended on killing Tom Gray.

THE END

Gray Redemption, the next chapter
in the series, is available
from Amazon.

About The Author

Alan McDermott is a husband, father to beautiful twin girls and a software developer from the south of England.

Born in West Germany of Scottish parents, Alan spent his early years moving from town to town as his father was posted to different Army units around the United Kingdom. Alan had a number of jobs after leaving school, including working on a cruise ship in Hong Kong and Singapore, where he met his wife. Since 2005 he has been working as a software developer and currently creates clinical applications for the National Health Service.

Alan's writing career began in 2011 and the action thriller *Gray Justice* was his first full-length novel.

Made in the USA
San Bernardino, CA
14 July 2014